Every Blade

of

Grass

Thomas

Wharton

ISBN 978-0-9939029-0-1

Cover photography: Jessica Christ

www.thomaswharton.ca

Other Books by Thomas Wharton

Icefields
Salamander
The Logogryph:
A Bibliography of Imaginary Books

The Perilous Realm Trilogy:
The Shadow of Malabron
The Fathomless Fire
The Tree of Story

In memory of Thomas Wharton Sr.

Every blade of grass has an angel that bends over it
and whispers, *grow, grow.*

The Talmud

1

When she went to check out in the morning she found a letter waiting for her at the front desk.

The only thing written on the plain white envelope was her name, but she knew right away who the letter was from. She stood holding the envelope, surprised at the emotions stirred within her by the sight of her own name in this unfamiliar hand. A giddy mixture of anticipation and dread she hadn't felt since high school.

Then it occurred to her he might be here in the lobby. Waiting for her to find the letter and open it. Watching to see how she'd react. God, like a stalker. *Please let him not be.* A quick glance showed her there was no one else in the dimly-lit, low-ceilinged room besides the few other journalists who, like her, were waiting for the bus to Keflavik airport. All men, they were huddled together like a herd of edgy muskoxen near the door, smoking and looking miserable at being forced out of bed at this ungodly hour. And it *was* early, though there was already light in the windows. At home it would have been pitch dark at this time of the morning but here, in summer, the sun never completely set.

She remembered then what he'd mentioned at dinner the evening before, that he would be leaving very early to join a sightseeing expedition to a glacier on the far side of the island. So no, he wasn't here. Good. He was on his way to see another wonder in this land of unexpected wonders. And in a few minutes she would be leaving. On her way home.

She stood hesitating at the front desk, uncertain whether she should read the letter now or wait until the next time she was alone. During the past week she had gotten to know many of the journalists on a first-name basis. Any moment now one of them would notice her and stroll over to wish her a good morning, then pointedly ask her who she was getting letters from in this out-of-the-way corner of the world. These people were relentlessly inquisitive. No, scratch that, they were as nosey as hell and always sniffing for a story. She knew it for a fact. She was one of them.

Damn it I've got nothing to hide, she thought, but quickly tucked the letter away in her carry-on bag before she went to join her colleagues.

On the shuttle bus she took a seat by herself and kept her head down, pretended to be searching through her notebook, hoping no one would sit down beside her. To her relief no one did, and the bus set off for the airport. After a few minutes she opened the envelope and slid out the folded piece of paper inside. It was lined, probably a page from that notebook he was always carrying around.

She held it unopened in her hand. Maybe it was best not to read what he'd written. Toss the letter in the next trash can she came across. Who knew what he'd written, or assumed. She hadn't been wearing her wedding ring all week. She'd stopped wearing it on assignments because too many people she interviewed noticed the ring and condescended to her after that. As if she wasn't a real journalist but a housewife who hadn't yet figured out where she belonged: in the kitchen cooking dinner for her man.

James Wheeler must have thought she was single. A mistake anyone could make. No fault of his, or hers. So why did she feel that unfolding this piece of paper would be like an admission of something? Of what, she wasn't exactly sure. She didn't want anything from him. She was happy with her life as it was. Reasonably so, which was all a person could expect in this world. She was married to a man she loved. She had a good job. She wasn't looking for an affair to complicate things.

Glancing out the bus window she saw that the sky had changed. The dull grey cloud cover had given way to a pale blue threaded with a few thin ribbons of red cloud glowing like hot filaments. It had rained every day this week, and now, on the day she was leaving, this glorious sunrise.

She smiled, glad for him, that he'd have a day like this. Then it occurred to her, she didn't *need* to read his letter. Which meant it was okay if she did. So why not just find out what he wanted to tell her, which was likely nothing personal after all. He was probably following up on one of the questions she'd been asking. There might be something here she could use for her article.

She unfolded the letter and read, surprised to find that her heart was pounding.

Reykjavik, Iceland

June 21 1974

Dear Martha Geddes,

When we were talking earlier this evening you mentioned you'd be flying home first thing in the morning. I wasn't sure we'd run into each other before then, so I thought I'd leave you this note. On the visit to Geysir yesterday the tour group was talking about wildflowers and I overheard you ask the guide if Iceland had any native orchids. He didn't seem to think so, but tonight after dinner I was talking with Professor Magnusson, who told me that the island in fact has eight wild species of orchid. Just thought you'd like to know.

I also wanted to tell you what a pleasure it's been to meet you. I came to this conference to talk with other ecologists about the greening of cities. I didn't expect to meet any journalists at this kind of scientific gathering, let alone one like yourself who seemed to be genuinely interested in what was going on here. I was surprised to meet someone in the media who was curious about the way the world really is, in its strange and surprising workings, rather than looking past all of that for the human interest story. During the past few days I was my usual inarticulate self— most of what I do is solitary field work, which doesn't give me much practice with social skills— but you always stayed to listen as I stumbled over my words. You are obviously very curious about the world and about people, and what is more, you didn't come here with a preconceived idea of what we ecologists do for a living. Usually when people find out I'm one of those "nature nuts," the response is hostility or baffled head-scratching. The result has been that I rarely look up from my research to notice the rest of humanity, since what I meet with is mostly misunderstanding. This past week, though, you made me look up and see things differently. Sitting here in the quiet of the hotel lobby tonight, writing this letter, I'm still looking up.

To thank you, then, in a way I think you will appreciate, I will close with the following: Professor Magnusson had a correction to the guide's assertion that Iceland has no reptiles or amphibians. The professor happens to know of a small population of frogs thriving near a geothermally-heated lake in the south of the island. He believes they must be the descendants of frogs rescued from dissection in biology class by some tender-hearted schoolchildren. At times the lake erupts in a burst of scalding hot water, and unfortunate individuals of this rare subspecies, the Icelandic leopard frog (*Rana pipens arctos*), can sometimes be spotted hurtling through the air. The professor first discovered this fact when a live frog dropped from the sky onto his hat.

Yours sincerely,
James Wheeler

She looked out at the stark moonscape of Iceland. The bare volcanic hills turning a blazing gold as the sun rose.

So that was it, then. Just as she'd guessed, he was following up on something she'd asked about. On a page from his field notebook. She'd been foolish worrying there might be something more.

... I'm still looking up.

She read the letter again. He had left his address at the bottom of the page. A city on the other side of the continent, in another country. So far away from where she lived. Another world.

Around her on the bus the other journalists were chatting, yawning, burrowing into their seats for a nap after a week of "white night" partying in the Reykjavik bars. For them this trip had been a chance to go wild in a place where no one knew them and to which they never expected to return. She overheard someone grousing to his seatmate about having spent a week on this drizzly, barren rock, and she remembered that her attitude hadn't been much different when she first arrived.

She closed her eyes and settled back in her seat. James Wheeler had been surprised at her questions, but the truth was, so had she. This trip to Iceland was her first major solo assignment since getting hired a year ago. Well, she knew the real reason she'd gotten the assignment: because no one else wanted it, and there was no way the magazine would send a woman to hotspots like Vietnam. She had arrived with one purpose: get the story of these far-out visionary scientists, then get back home. Show the editor she had what it takes. Five days ago, that was all that Iceland meant to her. A chance to prove herself. Then back to her own world, to her real life.

Then the man who had written this letter had shown her a glimpse of another life. He had praised her open-mindedness about things, but the truth was he'd helped reawaken it. He'd reminded her of a part of herself that she had almost forgotten. Something within her that had once been as essential as breathing, and that she'd been in danger of leaving behind and forgetting. The part of herself that needed nothing more than a sunrise to be flooded with well-being. With the knowledge that, despite everything wrong and compromised and hopeless in this mess of a world, being alive on the earth was still a miracle.

She thought about the visit to the geysers the day before. That moment when he'd reached to take her arm, to help her jump across a rushing meltwater stream, grey with glacial silt, and she had let him do it without a thought. So unlike her. She should have been offended at some man assuming she needed his help, but she *had* needed it. She'd been on tricky, unfamiliar terrain, her shoes were slipping on the wet rocks, and he'd simply reached out to give her a hand. He'd held her arm for a moment afterward, as if unwilling to let go until he was sure she had her footing. She smiled, remembering his look of embarrassment when it occurred to him he might have held on too long. And then it didn't matter in the slightest. Off she went, scrambling over rocks, jumping streams, climbing hills. She'd felt like a kid again, like the tomboy she once had been, off on another adventure. She asked him questions about the landscape and the wildflowers and he'd answered without condescending.

He was serious and thoughtful. He didn't swagger around acting like the world belonged to him because he had testicles, unlike most of the men she'd met on this trip. Unlike most of the men she knew, period. She had seen a calmness in the way he moved, a quiet physical confidence she had noticed in other men who spend a lot of time outdoors. She'd admired this in him, even as she told herself not to be ridiculous. But she had been drawn to him, she had to admit it now. Powerfully. Something had passed between them, she knew, even though nothing had been said.

The plane rose up through a bank of fog off the coast and she thought of her first trip in a passenger jet as a child, with her father. He'd given her the window seat and she'd sat with her face pressed to the glass as the plane went up and up. Watching the buildings and roads and cars get small like toys. How strange that had made her feel: excited and sad at the same time. Everything she knew changing into something tiny and far away. Then the view was gone and there was just a dim swirl of white and grey, and droplets of water appeared on the window, and then she'd realized what this was. Oh! She tugged her father's sleeve. *Daddy, look! We're inside a cloud!* Then they'd broken through into blazing light and this was the most wonderful thing of all: the silent shining white world on top of the clouds. Hills and valleys and forests of white, stretching on forever. What if you could just open the door of the plane and step out into all that light.

She didn't tug her father's sleeve this time. She just sat and looked.

As the plane headed out over the sea and Iceland disappeared behind them, she took out her diary and wrote

June 22nd

I've got lots of facts and anecdotes from the trip, but in no order. So much material and no clear theme for the article yet. Not sure what to put at the centre. Can't concentrate. Lack of sleep probably, thanks to the midnight sun. Making it difficult to focus.

She closed the diary, unfolded James Wheeler's letter and read it again. This time she smiled. She would write back to him. There would be nothing wrong in that. Nothing to feel guilty about. At the very least she had to thank him for the orchid fact, and the frogs. Yes, she'd write a letter and that would be it. But not now. She would find the right words after she got home.

She put away the letter and opened her diary again.

A lot to think about but I'll wait to start writing until I'm back on solid ground, where I belong. Not up here in the clouds.

New York, USA
June 26 1974

Dear James Wheeler,

I'm home now, plunged back into the welcoming traffic and grime of Manhattan, but some part of me is still back in Iceland, in that stark and beautiful landscape. My first night back home it was so strange when the sun went down and it actually got dark!

Thank you for relaying the fact about the orchids, and Professor Magnusson's tale of the Arctic frog. This is just the kind of strange little-known fact I can't resist. Here's another one: a birdwatching friend told me the other day that owls are the only birds that can see the color blue. I have no idea if this is scientifically accurate but I jotted it in my notebook just the same, as something to look up later. I guess I'm like another bird: the magpie, impulsively collecting curious odds and ends that no one else wants.

When I was a little girl I was sure I was going to be a ballet dancer. Then I was going to be a world-famous sculptor who would live in a driftwood cabin by the sea.

But as my notebooks kept filling with bits of fact and folklore I knew that I was going to have to work with words. I suppose I inherited this story-collecting habit from my father. He could strike up a conversation with anyone, young or old, and in no time have them telling all kinds of things about themselves and their lives. When I was a kid we spent our summers on Long Island. I still vividly remember the long walks Dad and I took together, how we would stop to chat with grocers, old fishermen, kids flying kites, and hear their stories. But he was an amateur naturalist and so he also had a story himself, about every tree or shell or oddly-coloured stone we came across. So that's where I get that habit.

Your letter was wrong about one thing—you are a fine storyteller. When our group went hiking in the hills that first day, it wasn't long before I realized that you were a person with a unique way of seeing the world. You stopped and pointed out things—the many colors of the moss and the lichens, the tiny Arctic blossoms and where they find shelter to grow. Things that the rest of us would have simply passed by without noticing. You knew the names of things, and how they fit together in subtle ways that I hadn't suspected. You made that unfamiliar world real for me, and you made me care about it. That is a great gift.

We obviously both travel a lot in our careers, and so I am sure we will meet again sooner or later. I look forward to that. In the meantime, here is a little-known fact in thanks for yours about the Icelandic frog. This is from one of my travel journals of a few years back. It happened on a boat cruise my husband Philip and I took down the Kwai River in Thailand:

Our guide caught a bat in a net tonight. A tiny thing. I got to hold it cupped in my palm for a moment before it flitted away. Dr Boonliang the naturalist says it's the world's smallest known mammal: the bumblebee bat. Craseonycteris thonglongyai (hope I got that right). These little guys were only recently discovered by science. An extremely rare species. An adult bat weighs less than a copper penny. They're apparently capable of hovering, like hummingbirds.

Sincerely yours,
Martha Geddes

Vancouver, Canada
August 6 1974

Dear Martha,

Thank you for the bumblebee bat of Thailand. I hadn't heard of this species before. I also look forward to our meeting again, whenever and wherever that might be.

We are having an arid, windy summer here on the coast. This is highly unusual for Vancouver, which usually gets a lot of rain. More than Iceland, I believe. Though definitely not as much of that relentless Arctic wind. Anyhow, as a result there have been many clear days here, so that from my front porch I've had terrific views of the summit of Mount Baker across the border in Washington, gleaming with snow. I've been told that this dormant volcano gets more snowfall than any other place on earth, or at least any place where snowfall has been measured.

About the colour perception of owls: I've heard it said that they can see *only* the blue and no other colour. I've since consulted an ornithologist friend of mine, and he says it's more likely that owls see the world as mostly black and white, the better to notice mice scurrying through the grass in the moonlight. Though even he doesn't know for certain.

Speaking of owls, I spotted a very elusive one not many days ago, on a small island in the Queen Charlotte archipelago, about five hundred miles northwest of here.

Our team of five researchers from the university got partway there by small plane and the rest of the way by motorized rubber raft. I'm not sure which mode of transportation caused the most stomach heaves. We were camped on the island for most of July, roughing it with nothing but a radio for contact with the outside world. The kind of isolation that some crazy ecologists live for. I have to admit I'm one of those.

I'm not a mystical person, pretty much the opposite, actually, but these islands can have an effect that's hard to describe in rational terms. Storms out of the Pacific strike the continent here first, in full fury, the waves battering the rocks with such earthshaking force that in the morning you climb out of your tent amazed to find you're still on solid ground. Or you can wake up to a bright, sunny morning and a minute later the mist will suddenly move in out of nowhere and blank everything out. Looking up you see the towering columns of cedar and fir vanishing into a gleaming haze. When you hike inland, the quiet stillness of the deep forest is a little unnerving. Or at least it seems quiet at first compared to the noise and activity of what we generously call the civilized world. But if you stay still for a while you hear things that were there all along, the faint stir and creak and rustle of a living forest, the sounds that make up what we urbanites call silence.

A friend of mine brought a tape recorder on one of our outings and we were stunned when we listened to it later and heard noises we couldn't remember hearing while we were there. We just hadn't tuned into them because we were focused on something else. These forest sounds seem to have more significance somehow, a deeper meaning than those you hear in the city, even if you're not sure what that meaning is, exactly. I'm probably reading too much into things at times like that. The result of spending too much time alone, probably. Sometimes I have the feeling I'm missing out on things that are supposed to be important to me. I'm 26 years old, my friends are getting married and having kids, and there I am sitting by myself in the woods.

Geologists believe that these islands were never glaciated during the last ice age, and as a result this is an ecologically unique zone, home to animals and plants that exist nowhere else on the planet. Like a subspecies of black bear with stronger jaws than the mainland variety, for cracking open shellfish. Or the Queen Charlotte saw-whet owl, which I caught a glimpse of through a pair of binoculars, after a rainstorm drew off and the sun came out. He was perched on a Sitka spruce branch hanging out over a cliff, at the bottom of which the surf was pounding and roaring. What he was doing there, and whether or not he could see the pristine blue of the sky, I don't know. I do know that he is, unfortunately, on the province's "blue list" of threatened species.

The islands are also home to the Haida people, who lived and thrived here for millennia, probably, before Europeans came along. When the trade in sea otter pelts began in the nineteenth century, smallpox and other diseases almost wiped the Haida out. Now they live in only two communities on Graham Island. The last time I was there I found a half-carved canoe in the forest, covered in moss. I nearly missed it, thinking it was just another fallen log. It's possible this canoe was left unfinished during the time of the epidemics, when the people who knew how to carve these vessels either died or abandoned their villages.

There's so much I don't know about this place, these people. I'm determined to come back one day, and stay longer.

About being like a magpie, I can relate. I carry index cards around with me everywhere I go. I jot any interesting stuff down, even if I'm not sure I'll ever need that particular bit of information. You never know, the odd behaviour of that owl could tie into something I'll be working on much later. The first lesson of ecology is that everything is connected, if you look long and carefully enough. When the cards start to get too bulky in my pockets I sort them by subject and store them in an old recipe box. I haven't always been that efficient: I just found that I was wasting too much time wandering the house looking for lost pieces of paper. I teach biology part-time, too, at the university, and eventually realized that students weren't happy with how often I misplaced their term papers.

One more little-known fact about owls. The feathers around their eyes act like little satellite dishes: they deflect sound waves to the owl's ear canals.

Best wishes,
James Wheeler

New York, USA
September 27 1974

Dear James,

Your description of the Queen Charlotte islands reminded me that I've never visited the west coast. I'd love to, one day. For the moment there doesn't seem to be any opportunity. Philip and I are so busy with work that whole days go by when we barely even see each other, let alone talk. Philip can be out the door before I get up, and sometimes comes home after I'm in bed. He is a radiology resident at St Luke's Hospital here in Manhattan.

It seems we have the opposite problem when it comes to age. I'm in my early twenties and my single friends sometimes lament that tying myself down like this so soon. They're afraid I'll start having babies and I have to ask myself, what would be so bad about that? It's odd that I would feel this way, I suppose, because my parents had me when they were both nearing forty.

I used to live in a rainy place—I was born in Dundee, Scotland. When my mother was little she lived with her family in Shanghai, but they fled when the Japanese invaded. I grew up with tales of the wonders of China and of the heroism of my paternal grandfather—he was a Methodist missionary there. When my mother was six years old my grandfather went on a journey into the interior, to meet and speak with Christians in other parts of the country. He never returned from that trip, and the authorities never found the slightest clue as to what might have happened to him. Some people suggested he was attacked by bandits, or was killed simply because he was a foreigner. There was a lot of anti-British sentiment at the time. Whatever the case, the family never discovered the truth.

When I was a little girl in Scotland I once had a particularly vivid dream about my grandfather. I dreamed that I was in a garden enclosed by a beautiful green flowering hedge, and that my grandfather was there with me. He had come to visit me, but he was a little boy. There is a framed photograph of him as a child at my mom's place— a very serious little boy looking right into the camera. This was that same boy, I knew in the dream. We played for a while at gardening, digging in the earth and planting seeds that grew into bright beautiful flowers, and then he stood up with this far-off look on his face, and it seemed to me he was both a child and an old man at the same time. He said *I have to go now*, and then he walked away from me. He passed through the green hedge and he was gone. I was alone in the garden. I could hear the keening of the wind as it wandered over a vast land on the other side of the hedge. I said to myself, *that's China*. There was a stepladder I could climb up on, to look over the hedge, but no matter how high I climbed, I couldn't reach the top. I couldn't see over. Then I woke up.

I've felt a strange longing for China ever since, although I've never been there. Philip's Uncle Henry tells me there's a word for that in German: *Fernweh.* Nostalgia for a place you've never been. Isn't that strange? I hope someday I'll be able to visit China. Not to search for answers about my grandfather necessarily, but to see this place where an important chapter of my family history was written. And maybe to find out why I have this longing for a land I've never seen. (By the way, have you heard about the ancient life-sized clay soldiers they've started to dig up in Shaanxi province? They were buried to guard the tomb of an emperor, and archaeologists say it's likely there's an entire army of them, thousands, waiting to be uncovered.)

We moved from Scotland to New York when I was eight, and I don't remember much about my birthplace beyond a memory of soft smoke-scented rain, and one particular incident: my maternal grandmother, Madeline (Maddie she was called by everyone) chuckling at me as I watched her roll a cigarette. I would have been very small at the time, since she died when I was five. I suppose I must have been staring at her like she was doing something magical—that's probably why she laughed. She smoked and drank whiskey in defiance of propriety all her life, God bless her. And she loved to dance. Family legend tells that when Maddie was a girl a stern older relation chastised her, warning that all this dancing would surely lead her one day into the arms of the Devil and he'd dance them both off to hell. Her reply: *Don't you know the Devil never dances? If he did he wouldn't be such a miserable bastard.*

Maybe it's from Grandma Maddie I picked up the smoking habit, although I've given it up recently. It doesn't seem to agree with me anymore.

I loved your description of the silence and the sounds of the forest. I read that part of your letter to Uncle Henry—I hope you don't mind—I knew he would appreciate it. Philip was pretty much raised by him after his parents divorced. He's the loveliest man—Philip thinks of him as a father. As do I. Anyhow, Uncle Henry, who calls himself an amateur kabbalist, says that there is a soul in all matter, not just in living things. When we knock on a wall, turn a page, break a glass, we are hearing the soul of an object speaking to us. Maybe that's why the sounds of the forest seem more meaningful to you than the sounds of the city—precisely because the sounds in the forest are less identifiable. You don't immediately assign a human meaning to them, and so the voice of the soul of things is clearer.

Anyhow, I'm definitely getting out of my depth here. As a scientist you probably think this is a lot of nonsense. And it does seem strange to talk about the soul of a place as I sit here with the window open, listening to the usual evening cacophony of traffic and sirens. All I know is that an ancient forest would be a welcome change. All you hear around this town is endless talk of Watergate and how New York City is going to hell in a handbasket (whatever that funny old saying means). The best I can do for a forest is Central Park. Which is pretty good, actually. You can get away from the city roar for a while, in certain spots. I've been spending more time in the park than I ever used to, and the truth is, I have you to thank for it. When I go for my daily walk now, I purposefully linger a little, to look for things I've never noticed before. My route used to take precisely twenty minutes. With practice, I'm hoping I can do it in thirty-five.

When I was a girl my father and I used to go hiking in the pine barrens on Long Island, and listen for bird calls we'd never heard before. I'm thinking of joining a group that meets here for "bird walks" every Saturday. They get up pretty early in the morning, but that's okay. I do too, these days.

All the best,
Martha

Vancouver, Canada
October 15 1974

Dear Martha,

Your Uncle Henry's theory about sounds is one I've never heard before. As a scientist I don't trade much in discussions of the soul of things. Still, I'll admit that after I read your letter I knocked on my desk and listened. I can't say I heard anything speaking to me.

The truth is, my skepticism about notions like this goes deeper than my scientific training. I'm not a believer in much of anything that isn't accessible to the senses or to the reasoning mind. I can't quite call myself an atheist, though, if only because it seems to me that kind of absolute, inflexible disbelief is just another kind of faith. I've known atheists who seem to have a real visceral hatred for this supreme being they claim not to believe in. Anyhow, since I've never seen any conclusive data one way or another about such things, I ignore it all as a problem science just hasn't found a way to test yet. Still, with everything I've learned about the laws of the cosmos and the formation of the Earth and our evolution from simpler life forms by the simple and perfectly explicable process of natural selection, my deepest instinct tells me this universe doesn't need a God and never did. What we do seem to need as human beings is a good story, and a loving creator with a divine plan for us is certainly that. An ancient story that has comforted and satisfied people for millennia. But for me, that's all it is. A story. A fairy tale. Something for anthropologists to puzzle over.

So there you have it. I don't mean to mock or belittle what your Uncle Henry believes. And I hope you're not offended. But I wanted you to know where I stand on this subject.

I hope you get a chance to visit China someday. I travel quite a bit, but that is one place I haven't been to yet. Nor had I heard about the clay soldiers. After reading your letter I did a little digging of my own in archaeological journals, to find out more. At the dig site they've found swordsmen and archers, standard-bearers, generals, and although the bodies were cast from molds, each face was sculpted to be unique, an individual. They'd been buried and forgotten, vanished from history for two thousand years.

I grew up about as far from rainy Scotland as you can get, on the bone-dry Canadian prairie. It was a pretty sheltered life. The kind of place where there aren't many surprises, and people like it like that. When I thought about my life at all, I guess I thought it was going to go on much the same. Until the day my mom died of a brain hemorrhage, when I was fourteen. She was walking down the street carrying a bag of groceries when it happened. Out of the blue. So we never got to say goodbye, or say any the things we would have said if we'd had time. It was hard on both Dad and me, of course, but to be honest after Mom was gone I couldn't wait until I was old enough to get away from the farm. I'd been your average outdoorsy kid up to then: playing baseball, exploring the woods and creeks with my dog, collecting rocks and arrowheads. But after Mom died I stayed in my room a lot and read books. Mom was a war bride, an Irish girl Dad met in England and brought home. She'd loved dancing and theatre when she was a girl. Her pride and joy, and her escape from farm life, was the piano in our front parlour. She used to sing and read poetry out loud in the evenings, too. I think that after she died I was angry that this hard, dusty farm life had taken so much from her, and then everything had been taken from her, far too soon. For a while I couldn't even stand to go into town, as if somehow this place itself was to blame for her death. I went through a period where I hated everyone there. In the evenings I'd go out drinking with friends and pick fights on the slightest provocation, fights which I usually lost. The books were my escape from all that anger, I suppose. Then they became a passion. Especially books about science. When I read Darwin's *Voyage of the Beagle*, I saw what an adventure science might be. How it provided a means to know the universe that one could test for oneself and so know to be fact, not superstition or wishful thinking. After that all I wanted was to know more, learn more, than I thought I ever would in a dead-end town like Rouleau, Saskatchewan.

Your letter was a reminder that there are amazing, unexpected things to find right outside one's door. I forget this a lot of the time. Too busy planning trips to far-off places, and endlessly writing grant applications to pay the way. In December I'm off again on another research trip, to the island of New Guinea.

Best wishes,
James

New York, USA
November 11 1974

Dear James,

My deepest sympathy on the loss of your mother. I know it happened years ago, but these things are always with us, in my experience. And I'm not offended by what you said about God and belief. I can't honestly say I know for certain where I stand on this subject myself. All I know is that I've had experiences that I can't explain, or even fully describe, and because of them, I believe there is more to this existence than the senses or one's reason can know.

I envy you your travelling. I have been staying fairly close to home lately. My dad died two years ago, and I have been spending a lot of time with my mother since then. She lives in a small cottage near the sea on Long Island. My dad was a self-sufficiency fanatic: if there was something that needed repairing or improving around the house, he would do it himself, and if he didn't know how, he would learn. Now that Dad is gone life is quite lonely for Mom, and she sometimes needs help with small repairs and such, not that she would admit it.

I look back now with an ache of longing for the hours I used to spend roaming the woods and the shore with my dad. How heedless I was of time back then. And I think it was precisely because I didn't care anything about the clock that a summer's day could be an eternity. Over the years I've let time become this resource that seems too valuable to waste on such trifles, and as a result there never seems to be enough time. When grown-ups tell children they're wasting their time doing nothing, they've forgotten this secret, that a whole world can unfold in an hour of simply *being*.

If only we could all keep that way of "just being" into adulthood. How much more time we'd find, within us and all around us. I like to imagine there would be time for a science, a field of study, of each individual thing. A science of particulars, rather than generalities. So for example a person who studied insects wouldn't observe a ladybug in order to learn more about ladybugs in general, but simply to learn about this particular ladybug, on this particular stalk of grass. Or that particular cloud. Or the raindrop that just landed on the back of your hand, the first one of a coming storm. But I suppose that's the opposite of what you scientists do, isn't it? Taking things out of context rather than finding out how they fit in with everything else. It wouldn't be science anymore, really, it would be something else I can't think of a name for.

Have a rewarding trip to New Guinea,
Martha

Surabaya, Indonesia
December 10 1974

Dear Martha,

I got your letter almost literally as I was heading out the door with my suitcases. I'm writing to you now from a hotel room without air-conditioning, listening to the patter of fat tropical raindrops on the palm leaves outside and feeling like I'm sitting in a steam bath. Too many raindrops to single out just one. But that's probably a wise way to begin a study of just about anything, to forget that it belongs to some larger group or class of things. Just see it for itself.

I think your father must have been a little like mine. He cherishes his independence and he's never remarried, although he's had a succession of lady friends. None of them have "stuck," as he puts it, maybe because Dad has his life ordered just the way he likes it and doesn't want his routine rearranged. And frankly he can be a grouchy old cuss, so there's that, too. His farm is a solid two days or more of driving from me, so I don't get out to see him as often as I would like. Though he doesn't seem to mind all that much that I don't. And he's never come here to visit. Too many damn people, he says. I spent a week with him last summer, poor timing on my part because he was in a rotten mood about a recent break-up with his latest girlfriend. He hardly spoke to me the whole time I was there, other than to mutter about the heat and the price of fuel and the goddamn feds in Ottawa and so on as if he was alone and talking to himself. If I tried to get in on one of these mumbled conversations I'd receive a grunt in return and not much else. One evening halfway through dinner he said, without looking up from his steak and mashed potatoes, "So, when are you leaving?"

That's just the way he is. I'm used to it and the truth is I find it oddly comforting. Sometimes a person doesn't really want certain things to change, even if they think they do. Before I left the next morning I gave him a hug and said "I love you, Dad."

His reply: "Yeah, well, I like you, too."

The enclosed photograph is of one particular Apollo Jewel butterfly that lives in the paperbark swamps on the coast of western New Guinea. The butterfly lays a single egg on top of a giant epiphyte called the anthouse plant. The plant grows out from the sides of trees like a huge, alarmingly spiky pineapple, and inside its thick stem live colonies of ants. The ants carry the egg inside the plant, where it hatches into a larva which proceeds to eat out more chambers for the ants to live in. They, in turn, protect the larva from predators until it is ready to cocoon and metamorphose into another Apollo Jewel.

I think that qualifies as a wonder.

There are so many things I could tell you about this place, I don't think I can confine myself to one single amazing fact. There's the paperbark tree, for example, the dominant tree of the New Guinea coastal lowlands. The bark grows in numerous thin, peeling layers on the trunk, which helps protect the tree during periods of flooding. The local people use the bark as an ingredient in cooking, as material for baskets and other containers, even as temporary shelters from rain and mosquitoes.

There is a species of cockatoo here that builds its nest in the hollows of trees, and fills the bottom of the hollow with twigs that it carries whole to the nest and then breaks up into smaller pieces. The eggs are laid on this twig layer, rather than in the actual bottom of the nest, so that during monsoon rains the newly-hatched chicks are protected from drowning.

If you trek inland from the paperbark swamps, as our group did a few days ago, you go through a steamy tropical jungle, a perpetually cloudy rain forest, a boggy highland, and finally you reach a snowcapped mountain range where there are glaciers that shine a faint blue in the sunlight.

Best wishes,
James

New York, USA
January 11 1975

Dear James,

Happy new year and thank you for the Apollo Jewel. I made room for him on my bulletin board and the truth is it took me a while to find space—I had to clear away several layers of clutter. But that's a good thing. I've been cleaning and tidying the apartment from one end to the other. My dear old family doctor tells me that this is what women do when they're going to bring a baby into the world. I wanted to argue with him, but instead I went home and got to work. Even though I'm not due until the summer.

I found my own office the toughest room to face when it came to readying the nest. But the Apollo Jewel has a spot all his own now. How lucky you are to visit places like that and see such things.

Have you ever seen the Haida canoe on display here at the Museum of Natural History? It's a magnificent thing, sixty-three feet long, carved from a single cedar trunk, and apparently seaworthy. The hull is only ¾ of an inch thick, and is decorated with a carving of a wolf and paintings of killer whales. There are wax models of Indians in the canoe, to depict the arrival of a chief and his retinue at a grand feast. I'm ashamed to admit that before your letter about the Queen Charlotte Islands, I had assumed there were no Haida people still living in the world.

I've been going to the museum a lot lately. And art galleries, too. I think I'm getting all of this out of my system for the day that's coming when my time won't be my own to do as I please. Another of my favorite exhibits at the Museum of Natural History is the meteorite that the Arctic explorer Robert Peary hauled back from Greenland. It's a massive thing, weighing over 70,000 pounds — he apparently had to make several trips there just to drag the thing all the way to his ship. They say the meteorite came from a proto-planet that broke apart during the formation of the solar system, over four billion years ago.

The museum actually lets people touch the meteorite. When you do, you're placing your hand on something as old as the sun.

There's an elderly woman who is well-known to the museum staff and to regular visitors like me. She comes there on Saturday mornings and talks to the meteor. Whether she thinks it's a sentient being that can relay her messages to another planet or dimension, I don't know, but I don't think that's the case. She just talks to it, about the weather, about her grandchildren, about her life. As odd as this sounds it really seems to me she does this out of empathy. She talks as if she *feels for* the meteor. I heard her say one time that it must have been so lonely during all those years of hurtling through empty space to get here. I suppose that if Uncle Henry is right about the soul in all things, maybe the old woman isn't so crazy after all. Anyhow I don't mind her, and I don't pity her. I might end up having conversations with inanimate objects when I get old, too. I've already noticed I've been talking to myself a lot more lately. Philip and I had some guests over for dinner the other night, a colleague of his and her husband. These were people I don't really care for—the kind that always have the right lamps, the right seats at the opera, the right breed of dog. Anyhow, I'd been writing all day and I was drained by dinnertime, and still half-absorbed in what I'd been working on, a piece about safety (or the lack thereof) on the subway. There was a lull in the conversation—the couple had run out of things to say about the right holiday they were taking next summer to the right beach in the south of France—and I sort of drifted away. Well, not *sort of.* I completely left the building. All of sudden Philip is asking me, "What did you say?"

I looked up, startled, to see all three of them staring at me. I'd been mumbling to myself, reworking a sentence that I hadn't quite managed to get right earlier in the day, something about commuters sitting on the train trying not to look at one another. Philip was embarrassed, I could see that, but I was more amused than anything. I'd given that couple the "right" anecdote for their next cocktail party. The nutty writer lady.

All the best,
Martha

From James Wheeler's field notebook
Jan 19 1975

Crossed south end of Fortress Lake on the way to the alpine cabin. Halfway across there was a groan from the ice and this weird low hum, like the vibration of a plucked electric guitar string. It seemed to zing around me from all directions then a moment later the noise just stopped. I stood there, didn't know what to make of it or what to do. A moment later distinctly felt the ice under my feet sink and rise again. Teetering, almost. Then heard the ice cracking some distance away, here, there, and that zinging vibration again. Ran for shore as if life depended on it, which it probably did. That likely wasn't smart, dashing hell bent for leather across the ice, but fear and adrenaline had taken over. Never experienced anything like this on lake ice before. Who to ask about it back at work?

Later at cabin re-read Martha's letter. She's going on with her life. I'm out here alone, as usual. Which is the way I like it, isn't it?

Vancouver, Canada
January 23 1975

Dear Martha,

My very best wishes to you and Philip.

    I've been to New York on a couple of occasions, and I went to the museum once, when I was twelve. I remember seeing the Haida canoe and Peary's meteorite. The meteorite is old, no doubt of it, but in a way it's no older than me, or you, or anyone else. All the protons in the universe, which make up most of the matter in galaxies and stars, and so of course the Earth and everything on it, including humanity, were formed at the first instant of time, the so-called Big Bang. I say "so-called" because when most people hear the phrase they imagine a massive explosion in the middle of the endless darkness of space, when in fact it was space itself that expanded at an unimaginable speed. As for what there was before space and time, if anything at all, who knows?

    Although the calendar tells me I'll soon be 27, it makes me a little dizzy to think that I should really be celebrating my 13.8 billionth birthday.

    I've just started a semester of teaching and when it's finished I'm off again, this time out to sea. I've signed on with a team studying gray whale migration in the Pacific. Word got to me through the scientists' grapevine that they needed an extra hand, and I managed to convince them that I know boats. I'm not sure why I was so eager to head out to sea. Maybe I simply haven't grown up yet and still want to be a pirate or something.

Wish me luck.

Your friend,
James

New York USA
May 4 1975

Dear James,

You're probably on your ocean voyage right now. I wish you a safe and rewarding journey.

Your last letter cheered me up about birthdays, which always make me a little blue for some reason. 13.8 billion years puts things like getting older into perspective.

Last Saturday I sat with my birdwatching group near the reservoir in Central Park. It was a fanatically early time to be up the morning, and pretty cold, but we were there shivering and sipping styrofoam cups of bad coffee for what turned out to be a good reason. Just before dawn, a green heron flew down out of the dark and skimmed the water's surface, then flapped its wings and rose again, as if it had noticed us at the last moment and decided to keep its distance. It came down out of the sky without a sound, touched the water with its wingtips and was gone. Only the ripples on the surface told us that it had really been there, that we hadn't all imagined it.

The city is right on the flight path these herons have been taking for millennia, so when they see the shine of open water amid the concrete sprawl, they head straight for it. A few days ago the bird we saw had been in the Amazon.

Warm regards,
Martha

Seward, Alaska
June 6 1975

Dear Martha,

Tomorrow morning our boat, the *Murrelet,* is heading home after almost three weeks bobbing around (like a murrelet, not surprisingly) at sea. It turns out what the crew needed was someone who can cook, and while I was a bit queasy just looking at food for the first few days, I was able to keep everyone fed. I didn't hear any complaints about the meals, anyhow. There are some compensations to the hermit life of a bachelor—you learn how to make meals.

We've been tracking gray whales as they make their annual migration north to their feeding grounds in the Arctic Ocean. The others scientists on board have been primarily interested in stragglers, groups of whales that, for some unknown reason, dawdle on the journey and arrive late. No one knows why. Maybe they just like to take their time. I can relate.

We got pretty close to a surprisingly large pod of females and their calves. The calves were up to fourteen feet long or so, and at thirty-six feet or so their mothers were almost as long as our (suddenly tiny and precarious) vessel. Several mother-and-calf pairs came right up to the boat and we reached over the side and touched them and petted them and rubbed their backs, as if we were all old friends who just happened to run into each other out here. They spouted into the wind so the spray gave us a good soaking — the spray from a whale's blowhole smells truly foul, I have to report — and it really seemed as if they'd done it in a spirit of fun.

As the whales surface sometimes their huge bodies move in a long slow roll, and then in the midst of this great heaving immensity there's a bright, aware eye regarding you with its own unfathomable intelligence. One of the other scientists said to me, "It's like looking into the eye of God." I thought that was a bit much, of course, but it is an impressive sight when they rise out of the waves – it sends a kind of exhilarated dread through a person.

As I mentioned, the first few days of the trip were pretty rough on my landlubber stomach. I was reminded of one of my heroes, Charles Darwin, who never got over his sea-sickness the entire five years he spent sailing around the world on the Beagle. He must have been tempted more than once to give up and take the first ship home. So I was feeling pretty proud of myself for sticking with it, just like Darwin. And then things got really interesting. One night a storm came up and tossed us around with such incredible noise and force that I went way beyond mere seasickness to something more primal. Sea-terror, you could call it. There I was down in the galley trying to stow things away, shouting and swearing and praying all at the same time. I definitely got the romance of the waves out of my system in short order. Fortunately we managed to keep boat, bodies and souls together, and last night I was well rewarded for all the misery — I saw something that few people have ever seen.

We were anchored off a small island, and in the middle of the night something woke me. I lay there for a while listening to the waves, but I couldn't get back to sleep, so I went up on deck. The sky was clear, except for a few swiftly-moving clouds to the west, trailing streamers of rain illuminated by the rising moon. This was a beautiful sight in itself, but as I watched, something else occurred that I had heard of, but had never seen with my own eyes.

As the moonlight shone through the drifting sheets of rain, a radiant arc began to form in the sky. All of the usual colours of the rainbow were visible, but much paler than those you would see in daylight. It seemed as if the earth had acquired a ghostly, serene ring, like Saturn's.

A few moments later the moonbow faded and was gone.

I had been too stunned to call the others, and when I told them the story a couple of hours later, they were skeptical. After all, we'd been celebrating the (13.8 billionth) birthday of one of the crew with several bottles of a brand of Polish vodka that could double handily as paint thinner. Someone asked me if I'd found a pot of gold at the end of this magical nighttime rainbow. Or just some pot. Someone else announced that he did have some pot, if anyone was interested. Several were, and the festivities started up again. I went back on deck. If people want to smoke that stuff it's fine with me. I just don't have any use for messing with my grey matter like that. The world is puzzling enough as it is.

If I believed in such things I'd almost have to say it was fate that I woke and went up on deck at just the right moment. And even though I knew full well it was a local phenomenon, visible only for a few miles, I found myself wishing you could see what I was seeing.

It's quite foggy tonight. The cabin window is open and I can hear a faint musical clang in the distance, a bell on a buoy or something like that, perhaps. Despite living by the ocean I've never been a very nautical person, but that seems to be changing.

I hope all is well with you.

James

New York, USA
June 16 1975

Dear James,

On the fifth of this month Philip and I welcomed our child into the world. We named him Michael, after Philip's beloved grandfather. He arrived at 3:15 in the morning and we soon discovered he has perfectly healthy lungs when he let us know quite loudly how he felt about making the trip. We are so happy, and so tired. The range of emotions one goes through in a short space of time is truly overwhelming. Fear, pain, anger, hysteria, joy, sadness, tenderness. And you lose yourself completely for a while, too. You get swept up in something much larger than yourself.

It occurred to me after rereading your last letter just now that the night Michael was born was the same night you saw the moonbow. So now you know what I was doing. I was too busy to be out skywatching, but I did discover a wonder. This baby is without doubt the most amazing little-known fact I have ever encountered, though I think I am getting to know him a little better each day.

Warm regards,
Martha

Vancouver, Canada
June 26 1975

Dear Martha,

I just returned from a conference in Seattle and got your letter with its happy news. My heartfelt congratulations and best wishes to you and Philip on becoming parents.

I didn't know whether you'd be allowed to plant a tree in Central Park, so I took the liberty of planting one here in Vancouver. The enclosed photo isn't very good, I know, but the site I chose is quite lovely. The tree is a Scots pine sapling, which I thought was appropriate. I planted it covertly, so to speak, with the help of a campus gardener who also happens to be a good friend, on a lawn overlooking the Strait of Georgia. Hiram, my gardener friend, says these are relatively slow growing pines, maybe one to two feet a year, but it should become a fine, sturdy tree some day.

A colleague of mine from Hong Kong tells me that the Scots pine (*song* in Chinese) is a symbol of long life in his homeland, and because the needles grow in pairs, it is also a symbol of married happiness.

With best wishes,
James

New York, USA
July 7 1975

Dear James Wheeler,

Martha told me about the tree you planted for our son and I wanted to thank you for the gesture. Neither Martha nor I have visited Canada but now we have a good reason to make the trip. My thought is that we should wait until Michael is old enough to understand that the tree you planted is for him, but Martha thinks otherwise. I'm horrendously busy at present — I'm involved with a massive cancer research project at the hospital, but you may find us on your doorstep sooner than you think if my wife gets her way.

Martha also shared with me some of the odd "facts" you've been exchanging. Great stuff. Where the hell do you get it — or do you just make it all up?

Thanks again,
Philip Gordon

P.S. Didn't mean to suggest we'd be asking you to put us up. We would just need you to show us where the tree is.

Vancouver, Canada
July 12 1975

Dear Philip,

Thanks for your note. I hope you, Martha and Michael will have a chance to visit Vancouver one of these days. When that happens I will of course be happy to take you to see Michael's tree.

And no, I don't make it all up. Nature does.

Best regards,
James Wheeler

From James Wheeler's Field Notebook:

In her first letter she called you a storyteller. And you have been telling a story. To yourself. A story about a man, a 26 year old ecologist from Vancouver just starting out in his chosen field. And a young woman, intelligent, charming, and graceful. Unlike the man she really enjoyed talking to people, drawing them out of their shells. She loved to laugh and see the odd and quirky side of things. The man wrote her a letter. She wrote back. It would be fair to say they became friends.

How did you think this story would end? It was always going to be like this.

Here's the story I want for her: the woman lived happily ever after.

And the man?

New York, USA
May 6 1976

Dear James,

It has been quite a while since we've exchanged news. I hope you are well. We are doing fine here.

"Fine" isn't quite the right word, actually. The fact is, I have been utterly swallowed up by this strange new state called motherhood. Michael is growing by leaps and bounds, and learning at an astonishing rate. It's incredible to Philip and me, but at ten months Michael could already say two words: "Mama" and "bird" (well, okay, it came out more as "boo") and now he's talking nonstop. We have a budgie in the apartment, Zazie, that he likes to chat with. The bird has been with us for a couple of years now, and hasn't learned a single word, but does a pretty passable imitation of a phone ringing. After Philip and I shared a bad cold a few months back, we noticed that the bird started making a sound very much like a cough. I almost got the feeling he was mocking us or paying us back for all the annoying noise we'd been making.

Michael was a small baby, but he has shot up over the last few months. I'd be interested to know if the tree is following suit. I've heard it stated as fact that children grow more in springtime than at any other time of year. That's my little-known fact for this letter, and I can attest to its truth.

I've been staying at home with Michael for a few months now. It means I had to give up my job at the magazine, but Philip and I decided Michael needs a fulltime parent more than I need my paycheck, such as it was. It also means I do most of my writing at home now, and to tell the truth, I love it. As it turned out I never did have much of a career as a roving journalist, but now I feel as if I'm on another kind of journey.

Here is our typical day: Michael usually wakes up first, VERY early. I feed him his breakfast and then he plays and I write (that's the ideal arrangement, anyhow). Then we have lunch, and I put him down for a nap, and write some more. Sometimes I can get an entire sentence polished before he wakes up again! Then we'll launch a major expedition to the park, to discover marvels unknown to one-year-old science, and then back home again for dinner. Often Philip won't get in until quite late, and so it will be Michael and I together for an entire day, just the two of us. Being a parent alone with a child all day must be something like the life of a monk. A monk withdraws from secular life, follows a daily ritual of chores, maybe tends a garden or does some other daily physical labor. With cloistered motherhood you've got the withdrawal from the outside world, the daily ritual, the tending of something beautiful unfolding before your eyes, and within you. Small, humble things can fill your heart. Something like the contemplative life, I imagine. "Contemplative" wouldn't be the first word one would normally choose to describe looking after a baby, but the truth is, sometimes even when Michael is awake and pulling things off the shelves or banging a wooden spoon on a pot, I can just be there with him and find a kind of stillness.

As my child learns to speak I've been reminded of a story I heard years ago, when I was a college student bumming around Mexico with my cousin, Nancy. I thought you might like it. I heard the tale in a beautiful little fishing village called Puerto Angel. One day on the beach Nancy and I met an old man who sold shells and driftwood carvings to tourists and got to talking with him. His name was Nestor. He told us that like many other people in his village he used to get much of his livelihood from the sea turtles that came ashore every year to lay eggs. The animals were slaughtered in the thousands, for food, and for also shells, meat and eggs to sell in the bigger towns. Nestor told us that during the nesting season there would be turtle eggshells and bones scattered everywhere on the sands, until the tide washed them away.

In time he began to notice that fewer and fewer turtles were coming back each year to lay eggs. So he and others stopped killing them. The turtles never came back in the same numbers they used to, he said, but they did come back. He was pleased about that.

We shared our lunch with the old man and he told us a story. I've dug out my journal from that trip and relied on my notes for the following version. I hope it's at least halfway faithful to what Nestor told us that day on the beach:

In the beginning, at the foot of the hill of snakes, the Maker stamped his foot on the bare, stony earth and a spring gushed forth with all the good things of the world.

One of these gifts was language but as yet no people had been created to speak it. We had not yet come out of our Mother the Earth.

The Maker bundled up all of this language and called his messenger, Coyote, to come to him. And Coyote came.

Behold, said the Maker, holding forth the bundle. *I have made speech.*

That's great, Lord! cried Coyote, even though he had no idea what the Maker was talking about. Coyote has always been a bit of a bootlicker that way. (And by the way, Nestor didn't explain how the Maker and Coyote were able to hold a conversation if speaking wasn't available yet. Maybe there was another form of communication in those first days).

The Maker commanded Coyote to take speech to the earth and find the People, the human beings who would be appearing soon and who would be in need of words with which to praise their creator. The Maker told Coyote what the human beings would look like, how to recognize them, and sent him on his way.

Now speech, or language, as the Maker conceived and planned it for us, was composed of many more sounds than those we know today. It was a great and awesome gift, and it weighed heavily on Coyote as he traveled the earth. He'd always been a bit lazy, if truth be told, and so he began to think about lightening his load as he went along.

Is it right, Coyote said to himself, *that a race of awkward, naked, two-legged creatures should get all of this wonderful speech for themselves?* The more he thought about it, the more convinced he became that this was just not a fair distribution of the Maker's great gift.

The first beings he came across were the winds and the waters. When he opened the bundle before them, the first sounds to leap out were great sighs and roars and thunderings. And that is why the wind and the waters speak with these mighty sounds.

When he had traveled on further, he again felt like easing his burden and so he gave what came next out of the bundle to the birds, and ever after that they have been able to sing and warble and trill like angels.

The Maker was going to give this joyful music, he marveled, *to mere human beings? Surely he can't have intended that.*

Coyote was so intrigued by what would come out of the bundle next that he started giving away sounds hither and thither to any creatures he met, and the results often brought him great amusement. He gave away grunts and squawks and honks and bleats and growls, until... nothing else came out of the bundle. Then Coyote saw that he'd gotten carried away, as he had so many times before, and now he was in some serious ... the word Nestor used was *mierda.*

In those days horses were the strongest and most fierce of the animals. No creatures hunted them, and all feared them. When they heard from the wind and the waters and the birds and animals that Coyote was giving away this awesome gift called speech, the horses set out to track him down. When they found him at last, making his slow, miserable way back to the Maker to admit what he'd done and beg for mercy, they surrounded him in a circle, their hooves striking the earth like lightning.

Coyote knew they were after whatever was in the bundle and if they didn't get it they would stomp him flat. In desperation he turned the bundle upside down and shook it as hard as he could. As luck would have it there was something left of speech. A very little something that had gotten lodged in the creases of the bundle and now finally came loose.

It was words. Good old blah blah blah.

The Maker was saving the very best of speech for you, great ones, Coyote said. *Here you go.*

Now that the horses could speak, they proclaimed themselves rulers over all the other animals. Coyote knew with a sinking heart that the Maker would find out about this in no time at all. He needed to come up with a cunning plan or he was doomed. Fortunately Coyote was a natural at cunning plans. He'd quickly snatched up another sound that had come bouncing out of the bundle along with those last bits and pieces called words. A sound that the horses hadn't noticed. A sound that just might save his hide.

He said farewell to the horses and started walking away on just his two hind legs. The horses thought he was crazy and jeered at him. Coyote halted and turned.

Oh, I'm sorry, he replied. *I should have told you. The Maker had decreed that from now on, in addition to speaking, all of us animals are supposed to walk on two legs like the human beings who are coming. The Maker wants all of us to be just like the human beings in every way. So you had better start practicing your walking.*

The horses talked it over. They knew that Coyote was the Maker's messenger and so they decided that even though he was known far and wide as a deceitful little cur they had better do as he said, just in case.

As it turned out the horses found it nearly impossible to walk on their hind legs and the effort soon exhausted them. While they lay there panting Coyote came up, rolled on the ground, and began to make a sound the horses had never heard before. It was the last sound to fall out of the bundle, the one Coyote had hidden from them.

Why are you doing that? the horses asked. *What is that?*

It wasn't a loud, frightening noise, not really. It didn't make Coyote sound dangerous, like a mountain lion's snarl would, or a bear's growl. But still the sound alarmed the horses greatly. It made them feel angry and ashamed of themselves, though they didn't know why. It hurt them in a place they had never felt pain before.

It's called laughter, Coyote said. *An awesome thing, don't you think? The Maker wants us to be like human beings, and this was the sound he was going to give to them. Only humans were supposed to be able to laugh. So we must put all our effort into laughing if we want to be just like them.*

The horses began to practice laughing, and in their haste to become masters of this terrible, powerful new sound, they cast aside words. And so, when they were busy with walking on their hind legs and laughing, Coyote was able to gather the words up again and shove them all back into the bundle.

After a while the commotion caused by the horses practicing their laughing and walking on hind legs came to the Maker's attention. He surveyed his creation and heard speech ringing out from every quarter, from the throat of every creature and every elemental power, and he knew without hesitation who to blame. In a rage the Maker summoned Coyote to appear before him.

Ne'er-do-well! Scoundrel! Wretch! the Maker thundered when Coyote appeared, slinking on his belly. *What have you done? My perfect silent earth is filled with clamor and the horses have gone mad.*

Coyote stammered out that somehow the horses had heard about speech and they'd forced him to open the bundle, and everything that was inside it had gotten out.

But please, Lord, don't be angry at the horses, Coyote added as he groveled. *They simply wanted to please you by learning how to speak and walk and act like the human beings that you're planning to favor so much.*

The Maker wasn't moved by Coyote's plea. He decided to punish the horses, and from that time forward the only sound they have been able to make is that desperate whinnying guffaw, that imitation laughter. As well the Maker saw to it that horses would no longer be fierce and fearless. He made their hearts so craven that it was easy for men to subdue them and make slaves of them.

Of course the Maker also suspected that Coyote had more to do with this sorry business than he'd let on, and so he punished him as well. He told Coyote that from now on he would have to make do with whatever sounds he could beg, scrounge or thieve from other animals. And that is why Coyote yips like the dog and howls like the wolf. But what the Maker didn't know was that Coyote kept a little of the laughter he'd been forced to hand over to the human beings along with words. And whenever Coyote encounters people and hears us trying to express our hearts to one another with words—those last feeble dregs of the bundle—he can't help but laugh to himself. If you've ever come across a coyote in the wild then you've surely seen the grin on his face as he slips away.

The story also tells that the horses were so ashamed of the embarrassing sounds they were left with that they fled from this land. But now they have returned to the Americas and it is said the horses chose to come. They sided with the conquistadors in their battles against the Indians because it was here, in the land that became Mexico, that they first suffered their humiliation.

Well, that surprised me. That story is the most writing I've done in a single sitting in weeks! (Michael's having an uncharacteristically long nap). Anyhow, that's more or less the story as Nestor told it to us. I may have embellished it a bit here and there in the retelling. It's a somewhat dark and sad tale, as Mexico itself can be, I've found, but I like the notion that the roar of the ocean is a sound human beings were meant to make. There are times in life, as Michael often reminds me, when words don't seem quite adequate to what we need to express. Anyhow, it just occurred to me who I was telling this made-up story to. I'm sure fables like this are of no interest to you, and maybe I should toss these pages away and start again, but I'm going to send it as is, maybe just so that I can prove to another person I've still got it in me to write.

Warm regards,
Martha

P.S. I'm hoping that this summer we will finally visit you and have a look at the tree you planted for Michael. I'm presently in negotiation with Philip over this!

Vancouver, Canada
June 25 1976

Dear Martha,

So glad to hear that Michael is growing and doing well. As is his tree. I went last night to check, and took a tape measure. The tree was 3' 4" when I planted it. Now, a year later, it has shot up to 4' 1". Not bad at all. I hope you will be able to visit this summer. I look forward very much to seeing you again, and to meeting Michael.

Thank you for the tale of Coyote and the origin of speech. I really mean that. Even I can enjoy a good story.

Now it's my turn to apologize for a long-delayed reply. I've been involved in some ongoing environmental issues that require a fair bit of traveling. It was good to hear from you and remember that there are things going on in the world that aren't completely mired in politics. I can't really imagine what it's like to be a parent, but your comments on the cloistered life reminded me of my fieldwork. Solitude, silence, and lots of repetitive labour. What a revelation — all these years I've been a monk!

I did make it to the Queen Charlottes for another visit. Things were not as quiet as they were the last time I was there. The residents of the two largest islands, Graham and Moresby, have started a protest campaign against the logging of the rainforests. They want a wildlife preserve set up, and in the meantime they've been chaining themselves to trees and staging sit-downs in government offices.

The logging companies had been telling people for years that the old growth forests were rotting, decaying remnants that needed to be cleared out and replaced with new, improved "planned" forests. Someone without a scientific background might look at moss-covered dead logs and think, sure, that makes sense. It was ecologists who took the time to study the old forests and discover that what looks, superficially, like a dying landscape, is really one of the richest and most complex ecosystems on the planet, one that is bursting with life. The logging companies do plant trees in places where they've cut them down, but the *forest* itself, the ancient web of life of which the trees are only a part, is gone forever. The people who live here knew this all along, of course.

Reporters from the Vancouver papers have been showing up to find out what's going on up there and I gave a few quotes from my perspective, which I knew would ruffle some feathers. When I got home there was a decidedly cool reception awaiting me from some of my more conservative colleagues in the faculty. These are people who know damn well what's at stake, but who refuse to speak out and risk their safe, comfortable niches.

Well, I didn't intend to go on like that, but on this subject I tend to get a little hot under the collar. The struggle over these islands is an important one, not only in and of itself, but also for the larger issue of how we hold stewardship over all such wild places. There aren't that many left in the world.

Best,
James

New York USA
July 7 1976

Dear James,

Your news about the Queen Charlotte islands was enlightening, and sad, too. I always imagined that part of the world as a pristine place. Which I suppose is another way of saying I simply didn't know anything about it. I hope the people of the islands succeed in getting their wildlife preserve.

Things have been exciting around here lately. Too exciting. I had a frightening experience with Michael a few days ago, just before the bicentennial. Philip was away at a conference in Boston, and I was at home with Michael, trying to finish a freelance piece I'd agreed to do, about community gardens in Manhattan. The work wasn't going well because Michael, who is usually quite happy to play on his own as long as we're in the same room, was restless, clingy and irritable all morning. By midafternoon he was no better, and when I checked his forehead I noticed he was alarmingly hot, so immediately I thought fever. I put him on the couch with a cold cloth on his forehead while I phoned my doctor's office to ask for advice (despite being married to a doctor I'm pretty useless when it comes to medical matters). The nurse told me to give him some children's Tylenol, keep him cool, and bring him in if things didn't improve. When I got off the phone to check Michael, he was limp and unresponsive and his skin had turned blue. Quite literally blue. I couldn't tell if he was even breathing. I panicked. I picked him up and carried him down the hall to my neighbor, a kind older woman named Ruth, who took one look at him and called for an ambulance. I was beside myself. It seemed ages until the ambulance arrived, but finally they came and took us to the emergency ward at St Luke's.

After an examination and a blood test the doctor told me that Michael had had a febrile seizure. His temperature had soared dangerously high as a result of an ear infection. I was stunned—I hadn't even suspected Michael had an earache, and I had no idea that these things could develop so quickly into something critical. Michael was given antibiotics and his temperature slowly came down, and after twenty hours in emergency, he was pronounced out of danger and I was able to bring him home. He recovered almost as quickly as he had gotten ill. Children are so amazing. After all the punishment his little body had taken he went right back to chattering and playing as if nothing had happened. I, however, was a drained and strung-out wreck. Philip came home soon afterward and I'm afraid I blew up at him for being away so often. I have a fairly stormy temper, which goes with the Scottish heritage, I suppose (sometimes I find it hard to believe I come from a long line of missionaries). Let's just say there wasn't a lot of peace and stillness in our little monastery that evening.

I've never admitted this to anyone else, but there are days when all I want to do is run away. I suppose every parent feels that way sometimes, when your world shrinks to dirty clothes, unwashed dishes, and cleaning mashed banana out of the carpet. I've come close to watching soap operas some days to escape from it all, God help me.

The truth is, sometimes my wish to escape goes deeper than this. Sometimes the world seems such a dark place that I wonder what I was thinking, bringing a child into it. As if the daily news about what human beings do to one another isn't bad enough, there are all the problems that scientists like yourself are alarmed about. Since we've been writing back and forth I've paid more attention to what's going on with nature and the environment, and I've begun to see how the conflict in the Queen Charlottes you've described is everywhere. The human population continues to grow, and more and more of the natural world gets despoiled in the name of money and progress. Where will it end? How can it end, other than in more and more people fighting over less and less of the planet's bounty. I want to take my child and find someplace safe where these things aren't happening. But there is no such place. At moments like that I confess I don't have much hope for the future, and that frightens me.

To cheer myself up on Independence Day I took Michael to see the fleet of sailing ships from around the world that were coming here for the bicentennial celebration, so we got our act together. A friend of Philip's lives on Riverside Drive in a fifteenth-floor apartment overlooking the river, and he invited us over to watch the spectacle. Michael and I had a magnificent view as the ships came up the Hudson. I think the swarms of people lining the shore and every other available vantage point were almost as incredible to see as the tall ships themselves. We arrived at our friend's place early in the morning, when it was wet and gusty, and watched as the crowd along the riverfront grew and grew until it looked like a horde of lemmings. Fortunately there was no mass plunge into the water (although from what I understand, that's just a myth anyhow).

The rain finally drew off and the tall ships appeared under full sail, surrounded by a fleet of American naval vessels. The sun came out fitfully and the sails and the rigging flashed and gleamed. The best word to describe it is *bracing.* The sailors waved flags from the decks and then the crowd simply erupted into a roar of cheering and waving. What were we all getting so carried away for? I doubt anyone there could have said for sure. Maybe over the years we had forgotten that New York was a port city, with all the bustling life and excitement that fact brings with it. The ships made us see the magic of our tired old city again. For a little while, the world felt like a place of promise.

All the best,
Martha

Vancouver, Canada
July 23 1976

Dear Martha,

I'm glad to hear that Michael and you came through the fever unscathed and well. It must have been terrifying for you both. I remember the fevers I used to get every so often as a child. You feel as if you're at the mercy of gigantic, incomprehensible forces—nothing in adult life comes close to it, I imagine.

What you've said about lack of hope for the future is something I deal with on almost a daily basis. A colleague of mine who studies industrial pollution says that if it wasn't for the bright young people he's met who want to make a difference, he would've blown his brains out a long time ago. I can't say I've ever felt quite that desperate. Close to it sometimes, maybe. When I get gloomy about the future I remember something my Mom said to me once when we were picking berries one day.

"Isn't it something," she said, holding up a bright red raspberry, "the way they come back every year, good as new. Why do they bother? Our priest used to say that God made all of this just for us. For human beings, because we're the jewel of creation. I never believed it. I mean, look at them, Jim. These are the jewels."

I'd never heard her say anything like that, and I never forgot it. Just a few words, but they cross my mind almost every day. I suppose they remind me to appreciate what's right in front of me, in the here and now. And that even if people don't come back, life always does.

I don't know if it will be of any help to you, but here is what I know unequivocally to be true: life on Earth began with an original single-celled organism, probably very much like the cyanobacteria that exist today. Over millions of years this one primitive, tiny ancestor branched out, as Darwin put it in *The Origin of Species,* into "endless forms most beautiful and most wonderful." We humans believe we're separate from other creatures, but we are what that first tiny spark of life eventually became. Along with every other living thing that exists, and many species that no longer do. Life has suffered catastrophic losses during Earth's history, but it has always carried on and flourished again, and found new forms. I don't meant to say evolution has a purpose, that it's working toward some predetermined goal, for example us. It isn't. If conditions had been different, human beings might never have been. But here we are, one of the many filaments of that single thread that began so long ago. In all these unimaginable eons, through all the struggles against nature's implacable forces, the thread of life has never been broken. Living things have lived and vanished, but *life* has never died.

This will sound strange I suppose, but I take comfort and inspiration from that thought.

Best wishes to you and your family,
James

New York USA
August 6 1976

Dear James,

Thank you for sharing your mother's words. They touched me deeply and helped lift my spirits.

I was surprised by the way you talked about evolution, about how it has no goal. I suppose if anyone had ever asked me what Darwin's theory was or how it worked, I would have responded with the old saying that it's all about the "survival of the fittest." Then I probably would have conjured up vague memories of high school biology to talk about how life developed from primitive mindless crawling things to more complex and "better" forms, with human beings as the ultimate end result, the cream of the crop.

What you're saying, if I understand correctly, is that we're here not because nature had a plan but because it *didn't.* Life took the only paths it could, the ones that allowed it to keep going. Which leads me to wonder what paths will close or open for life in the future? Well, specifically for us. I have to admit the thought scares me a little, living in a universe that doesn't care if human beings continue or go the way of the dodo. Or the girdle. But if it's true then it also means we live in a universe where the future hasn't been written, and never will be. Life will always be open to the new. Which, come to think of it, is a good way for a person to be, too.

All the best,
Martha

From James Wheeler's Field Notebook:

August 11, 5:15 PM: Coquitlam River meadows: a large orbweaver's web spun between two cattail stalks. In it a blue and gold dragonfly, its body vibrating helplessly. On closer inspection: spider on the dragonfly's neck, either delivering a paralyzing bite or already sucking out the juices. Spider motionless. Looks like it's giving the dragonfly a long, intimate kiss.

Unusual: the orbweaver hadn't wound its catch up in a cocoon of webbing before beginning its meal. Another unusual fact: there's a fly in the "cage" of the dragonfly's legs, which are still feebly trying to lift its own dinner toward its jaws.

One of those moments that reminds me why I didn't become an entomologist.

Later: thinking about Martha's last letter. Surprised by what she said about the future not being written. Open paths. Never thought about it like that. I told her I was inspired by life's resilience but could have just as truthfully told her that there are days like this one when life seems nothing but a pointless, mindless struggle. Eating and being eaten. All the billions and billions of living creatures that have been born, that have existed briefly and died, like that dragonfly, all for the sake of passing on their genetic instructions. Or failing to pass them on. And all of it meaning nothing and going nowhere, ultimately, except oblivion, when our sun dies and the Earth is burned to a dead coal.

But here we are, these curious, troubled apes, wondering and dreaming and wishing. What was the adaptive value of the little spark of self-awareness lit in a primate's brain on the savannah a million years ago? How does looking up at the stars and wondering what this world is and why you're here help you catch an antelope? Why do some of us wander around out here in the woods, scribbling notes about spiders and dragonflies, when we should be doing what all of the other creatures are doing, getting busy passing on our genes like nothing else matters?

From Martha Geddes' diary

Sept 2 1976

Philip finally admitted he'd slept with that woman. I sat and listened while it all came out, or at least as much as he thought I should hear. I was sitting beside the Christmas tree and the light reflecting off this one glass ornament as it turned was winking at the corner of my vision and I kept glancing at it. As if what Philip was saying didn't matter as much as the light on that ornament. As if this was happening to two other people, not us.

Philip stopped talking, and then he started crying. He said the things men say in movies, about how she meant nothing to him, it was a mistake, he's learned his lesson. I thought about how it took him over a year to learn that lesson. He had to keep going back to her for further study I guess.

I wanted to laugh, cry, scream. I didn't do any of that. But I didn't want to be in this sordid little movie, either. I got up without saying anything and went down the hall to check on Michael. Then I went to my room and shut the door. I heard Philip leave.

That's when it started. I had to hide my head under the pillow so the noises I was making wouldn't wake up Michael.

Heartsick. Almost morning now. I don't know what to do. I want to take my child and be gone when Philip gets back. I want to go to sleep and wake up and have it all be nothing but a bad dream. I want to stop thinking and writing these clichés of the cheated-on wife. I can't sleep. Michael will be waking up soon. I don't know what to do.

New York, USA
September 30 1976

Dear James,

The summer is over and we haven't made the trip to visit you and to see Michael's tree. The truth is I'm in the midst of something difficult that I can't see the end of. Please forgive this weak excuse. All I can say is that I envy the solitude and quiet you're able to find in your work. I could use some of that about now. Someday we will make the trip, I'm determined on that. But for now there's just no way.

It's a shame that your teaching methods face such narrow-minded opposition. I suppose none of us can escape from these sad, pointless power games at work or anywhere else. I wish you the best of luck in the fight for Persephone Island.

Best wishes,
Martha

Vancouver, Canada
October 9 1976

Dear Martha,

There is nothing to forgive, and no need to explain. In my line of work I've had to learn patience. Whatever it is that you're in the midst of, I wish you well and hope you quickly find your way through it.

I'm afraid I don't have an amazing fact for this letter, either. Just a plain and simple fact, that if there's anything I can do to help you, I will.

Your friend,
James

New York, USA
April 4 1977

Dear James,

How are you?

It has been a long while since we've exchanged news.
I hope you're finding time to get away from department
meetings and into the forest.

I never thanked you for your last letter. I want you to
know that your support and friendship has been a great
help, and I feel I owe you more of an explanation. Philip
and I have been going through a difficult time in our
marriage. I can't say that everything has been resolved, and
I honestly don't know what the future holds. Which is
something I remember feeling good about in a previous
letter: that the future is unwritten. The truth is I could use
a well-written ending right now. Or at least a new chapter.
But lately I'm more hopeful, about a lot of things. It's
helped that spring has come and we're able to get out of
the apartment more often and breathe some fresh air.

Remember that community garden piece I was working
on? It really sparked my interest in the world of gardening,
and through an acquaintance who's moving out of state
I've managed to "inherit" a small space in one of these
plots. Now I am feverishly reading everything I can get on

the subject, in preparation for diving into seeds and bulbs and soil with trowel at the ready. I've just started seeding — if my crops actually grow, I'll have carrots, beans, squash and lettuce. I've also got some tomato plants growing in pots on my balcony, alongside the no-hassle cacti I've had with me since college days. I've also planted flowers. A few perennials, asters, irises and delphiniums, but mostly annuals: sunflowers, pansies, calendulas, morning-glories. That way, if I don't like how things look this year, I can try different arrangements next year.

Michael and I go regularly to inspect our vast estate. I put Michael in charge of watering, a responsibility he takes very seriously. Often he lets me take the watering can, though, because he's discovered that supervising can be even more fun. He likes to correct me if he feels I've watered too much or too little, even if it's only a drop or two. This despite the fact that we're still waiting for something green to turn up.

The other day we went out to my mother's place, and after dark I took Michael down to the seashore. I was thinking about the story I'd heard in Mexico — about how Coyote gave speech to the wind and the waves — and it occurred to me I might be able to hear this speaking better at night, when there wouldn't be a lot to see and thus fewer distractions from simply listening. It was a wet, gusty night, and the ghostly grey breakers were crashing up out of the dark, the froth spraying up at us. Michael was a little frightened at first, but I cradled him in my arms and we stood together on the brink of this dimly-seen tumult and let it come at us with its full force and mystery. Of course I don't know what Michael was thinking and feeling, but he seemed to be in a state of relaxed alertness, calm but paying careful attention with all of his senses to what was happening around him. I'd like to think he will remember this night years from now, or that in some subtle way it will simply become part of who he is. I love to watch his fresh, innocent reactions to all things new and unfamiliar, and yet I'm also eager to meet the man that he will grow to be. That night at the seashore I felt as if I had a glimpse of him, the grown-up Michael I mean, and I was filled with a kind of joyful sadness, you could say. I saw myself as an old woman with my grown son standing tall beside me, looking out after many years at the same eternal spectacle of the waves. It might just be a mother's fondness, but at that moment I felt certain he would grow up to be a good man, and that experiences like this would help to make that so.

I'm writing again, working on short pieces about gardening, and the city during different seasons. People seem to like them.

Best wishes,
Martha

Vancouver, Canada
April 19 1977

Dear Martha,

It was a treat to come home from a long tiring day and find your letter. I should have taken the time to write more often lately, but the battle for Persephone Island goes on, as does the dance at work with the anti-tree-climbing faction. As a grad student in the Sixties I was mentored by a controversial professor who was more or less hounded out of his position, and according to some good friends I've been targeted for a similar campaign. When I first heard about this I laughed it off. I thought that if I ignored the whole thing it would just disappear. If only it were that easy. Every night I come home drained and more fed up than ever.

It sounds to me like you've had similar experiences with politics at work. How do you deal with this kind of thing? It feels like I'm being eaten, slowly, in tiny little bites. Fortunately I'm taking a short trip to the Arctic in the summer with a geologist friend of mine. I hope to recharge my batteries a bit while I'm there. Solitary places always seem to do that for me.

Let me know how your garden turns out.

Your friend,
James

New York, USA
July 16 1977

Dear James,

I sympathize with your difficulties at work. There are various ways to cope. One is of course to bite back, but I wouldn't recommend that. It can be taken for panic and throw the opposition into a feeding frenzy. You used the word "dance" in your last letter, and I think that's a good way to look at it. Work conflict as an art form, in which you have to be graceful, nimble, and quick to respond. I remember one office job I had where the mood was particularly toxic. When things got really bad I used to pretend—in my own head, I mean—that I was in a Broadway musical. I'd look at the dour, hostile faces around me and imagine everyone suddenly bursting into a big song-and-dance number from a musical like *Anything Goes* or *A Chorus Line*. "They say that bears have love affairs, and even camels. We're merely mammals, let's misbehave!" An image so incongruous it would keep a smile on my face for the rest of the day.

I've started writing short articles that my editor calls "that science stuff." He wants me to write a regular feature based on my birdwatching, but also other observations about nature, seasons, the workings of the human body. I've been inspired by your example, really. Enclosed is a piece I wrote recently about the other living things that make their home on us and in us, the skin mites, the *trillions* of bacteria, the viruses. It makes you see yourself in an unflattering light. Writing it, I was reminded of a cautionary tale Uncle Henry liked to tell about his neighborhood butcher, a kind, patient man he admired. Into this butcher's shop one day came Mrs Katzman, the world's fussiest customer. True to form she started minutely examining a chicken. She squeezed it, prodded it, turned it every which way, spread open its legs and peered inside. Finally, with a shake of her head she declared this particular chicken no good.

"Mrs Katzman," said the butcher softly, "could you or I pass such a test?"

Which reminds me of another change in my life to tell you about: I've become a vegetarian. It came about while working on my garden. I started thinking more and more about what I eat, what we eat as a family, as a society, and after doing a lot of research about nutrition and health and so on, I felt it was the right choice. For me, that is. I didn't make it a requirement for anyone else in the household. I doubt Philip will ever join me in swearing off sirloin steaks and chicken Kiev and such, and Michael can make his own choice if and when he likes. I'm not guilting anyone else into this and or trying to convert them. Truth is I did some backsliding before I managed to completely abandon my carnivorous past. I couldn't resist a burger now and then at company picnics, that sort of thing. Anyhow, dinnertime these days often finds me wracking my brains trying to come up with both a meat dish and a vegetable main course. And when we go out to someone's house for dinner, or I eat lunch with co-workers, people have been discovering that I no longer eat meat, which makes for some awkward moments and some condescending or even angry reactions, along the lines of *oh God, she's really flipped her lid.* Or even *so you're better than the rest of us now?* It turns out some people don't really understand what the term *vegetarian* actually means. The other night we were invited for dinner by a work colleague of Philip's and when his wife brought out the main course, a delicious-looking tagliatelle with peppers and steak slices, she had a separate dish for me.

"I heard you were a vegetarian," she said as she set the plate in front of me, "so I cut your steak into really small pieces. You won't even notice."

Speaking of plants, the garden had a fine, encouraging start. I was shocked at first, then I made sure that Michael knew our success was due in large part to his deft hand with the watering.

It was a good start but the recent heat shriveled up almost everything in our community garden except the dandelions. It has been almost literally one hell of a summer here in New York. People have lost their jobs in record numbers, services have been cut, the city is broke, and we've been broiling in a heat wave that's lasted for days on end, with temperatures well into the hundreds, dropping people like flies. On top of that, as you've probably heard, the police have been desperately trying to track down this "Son of Sam" before he murders any more innocent people.

And then, when we were asking each other how on earth it could possibly get any worse, we got an answer: the blackout.

Philip was at work that evening. Michael was asleep, the air conditioner was humming away and I was reading a book when the lights went off, and there was complete and utter silence. I found the flashlight and checked on Michael, then lit some candles and went out onto the balcony to see what I could see, which was the most startling, profound darkness. The downtown skyline had been swallowed up, although after a few moments I could just see the faintest suggestion of the Trade Center towers, two black monoliths against a slightly grayer dark. It was then I realized how reassuring a sight the towers had come to be for me. Like just about everyone else in New York I disliked the towers on principle when they went up -- great big phallic symbols of hubris and excess, etc -- but over the years they became permanent features of the landscape, like familiar tall trees: there they are, as always, enduring like the rest of us.

Michael woke up—it may have been the absolute silence that did it—and started calling for me, so I got him out of bed and took him out on the balcony. As we stood looking into the dark, the sirens started wailing, and then came the sounds and sights of people gathering in the streets. At Philip's hospital, where he and the other medical staff worked nonstop through the night, emergency surgery for the injured was performed in the parking lots with lights supplied by generators.

The streets of Greenwich Village, not surprisingly, filled up with an impromptu festival. And orgy, from some of the stories I heard. And I'm sure you've heard the other stories, too, about the looting and burning. For a while this city was like something out of a Hieronymus Bosch painting. Well, that's not quite accurate. On an ordinary night this town is like something out of a Hieronymus Bosch painting. This was pandemonium on a whole new scale.

I was scared, I'll admit, a lot more than Michael was, but there was something exhilarating about the darkness, too. As if a giant noisy machine that made it hard to think had been suddenly shut off, and a planet you had never seen before was revealed. Michael and I had all the stars above us, too, for the first time, with only a thin sliver of moon. I think you would have liked it.

I couldn't impress Michael with the Milky Way, unfortunately (he only just turned two) but since I had never seen it before I just kept looking up and looking up until my neck was stiff and sore. For a long time all I could see was what I expected to see, the stars, but then, after I had tried tracing out some constellations, mostly unsuccessfully, I suddenly saw what all those tiny, glittering points of light were shining in. I mean, I was aware like I never have been before of all that emptiness. How those frail beams of light come to us across billions upon billions of miles of silent, cold darkness.

I don't know why but I got to thinking of my friends, both near and far, and I felt more than ever how grateful I am for the light they send me. I hope once in a while I manage to send some back.

All the best,
Martha

Vancouver, Canada
July 29 1977

Dear Martha,

The light has been received, and the article on the body. I enjoyed it very much, and yes, it's *science* as far as I'm concerned. The object that accompanies this letter is a small token of my thanks for sending it, and for your good advice regarding stress at work.

It looks like nothing more than the cracked-off half of a good skipping stone, but on the broken face, if you look carefully, you'll see a hair-thin band of green, among the darker grey striations. This thread of green is actually a living thing, a kind of lichen called a cryptoendolith.

The stone comes from the Arctic research station on Ellesmere Island where I was staying earlier this month. I have a personal rule against removing specimens from the places I visit, but I ignored it just this once because the rock, I was told, had already been sitting on a windowsill at the station for years, and no one seemed to mind my claiming it.

I didn't have much to do while I was at the station, other than roam around looking at lichens (while keeping one eye out for polar bears). But I suppose that's just what I needed — a few days of doing nothing much at all. Anyhow, it meant I had plenty of time to poke around in the corners, and this stone is what turned up.

Like any other lichen, the cryptoendolith is a symbiotic colony formed by bacteria and algae, but this lichen is even more unusual: it lives inside rocks. Incredible how tenacious life can be in its efforts to carve out a niche for itself, even in the harshest terrain. The cryptoendoliths grow just under the translucent surface of a rock, where there's enough light and trapped humidity for photosynthesis to take place. When the climate takes a turn for the worse the colony goes into suspended animation, literally freezes, sometimes for hundreds of years, until conditions become favourable again for life and growth.

There are cryptoendoliths making a go of it in the Dry Valleys of Antarctica. Someday I hope to go there as well and have a look at them.

Care of the cryptoendolith is simple. You can just leave it on your desk or on a bookshelf and it should be fine. Consider it my humble addition to your garden.

I know the blackout was a terrible event in a lot of ways, but I can't help envying you for having seen it first hand. You're right, I would have liked to have been there. Since reading your letter, I've been imagining what it would be like if the same thing happened here in Vancouver. For a while the night would be as it once was before Europeans set foot here. I would like to experience that.

"Scotty" the tree has reached 5' 9'' this season. Looks like I'm going to have to bring a ladder with me next year.

Congratulations on going vegetarian. I haven't eaten meat for years but it started as an almost unconscious thing, really. Being away from home a lot I rarely bothered to make full meals. Usually I just grabbed a quick salad for lunch at the deli. After a while I noticed I was always heading for the vegetable trays and wasn't interested in the cold cuts anymore. Couldn't stop thinking about the fact that this was decaying muscle tissue from what had been a living animal only a short time ago. But I rarely talk about my eating habits, pretty much for the same reasons you give. I got tired of the sarcasm and misunderstanding.

I'm sad to report that the battle for Persephone Island has not been going well. I won't go into the byzantine complications of all of this, but our coalition of conservation groups just lost a court challenge. We can see an awareness and real concern for what we're doing to these irreplaceable forests is growing among people, even some in the logging industry. Unfortunately it hasn't grown strong enough yet to tip the scales. Still, I have to believe people will wake up one day to the fact that we came from nature and we absolutely depend on it for our very lives. A *we* that includes everything that lives in us and on us.

Your friend and fellow ecosystem,
James

New York, USA
August 10 1977

Dear James,

Thank you for the cryptoendolith. I hope caring for it won't prove to be beyond even my meager gardening skills.

I'm sorry to hear that things have not gone as you hoped with Persephone Island. On a much smaller scale, there are similar battles going on here between the developers and those of us who prefer our community gardens to yet another office tower. There's one way, I suppose, in which we're fortunate not to have acres and acres of untouched green space on our little island. It means that the little we do have is loved and held as precious beyond any price, for its own sake. And that means a lot of people are willing to fight long and hard to preserve it.

I'm writing to let you know that my cousin Nancy Heywood will be coming to Vancouver in September to attend graduate school. She's working on a Master's degree in English literature. When she saw your photo of "Scotty" with the sunlit blue ocean in the background, she decided she'd had enough of dangerous, dirty NY and was going to try life in far-off British Columbia, where they have fresh air and muscular lumberjacks. I gave her your address — I hope that's okay. Be prepared, she's a live wire. You may feel like a tidal wave has hit town.

Warm regards,
Martha

P.S. Last week I was in Maine to cover the lobster festival in Rockland. Which was hilarious, given that I wasn't going to eat any of the catch. But my boss didn't know that, and I needed the assignment.

Philip came with me. We went out walking along the shore one evening, to have one of our long talks. It didn't go so well, so I thought I'd show Philip what Michael and I had shared earlier this year, how we listened to the roar of the waves and felt the ocean before us like a living thing. This time around, though, the sea was quite calm, and there was a sliver of moon. As it happened, the quiet gave us the opportunity for a long overdue talk about many things. After a while we noticed a faint blue-green glow out on the ocean. I've heard it said that this kind of light at sea is caused by some kind of microscopic animal but I haven't been able to track down the name of it, so my little-known fact for this letter must remain incomplete.

Vancouver, Canada
August 16 1977

Dear Martha,

I look forward to meeting your cousin Nancy. Please tell her that I'm happy to help her get moved in and find her way around.

The single-celled creature that produces lights at sea is called *Noctiluca*, which fittingly means "night light." It is found in all the world's oceans in vast numbers, and gives off bioluminescence when disturbed by wave agitation from wind or the plowing movement of ships.

Nobody is sure what purpose this light serves, though one possibility is that it attracts other photosynthetic single-celled organisms, upon which *Noctiluca* feeds. This living flashlight has a long flagellum, a whip-like appendage which sweeps other microscopic creatures into its feeding pouch.

I wouldn't be concerned about your fact remaining "incomplete." They all do. We humans haven't finished writing the book on nature, in fact we've just barely started. Which is why I'm not out of a job yet.

Your friend,
James

Vancouver, Canada
September 19 1977

Greetings from the wild side of the continent!

Well cousin I'm settled now in the great northwest and starting classes. Okay I'm not quite *settled* yet (have I ever been?). Still getting used to really actually being here. It's been raining almost nonstop since I got off the plane. Seriously. That's a bit of a drag, but the air is so soft and mild. I don't know quite how to describe it to you. Maybe it's the quiet, too, on the tree-lined sidestreet where I'm living now. In the short time I've been here I've already learned something I don't think I could ever have learned back home in the grimy city—you can actually *feel* the quiet on your skin. Like an easing up of pressure. Or maybe I've just gone nuts. Probably. Anyhow, last night (when it stopped raining for ten minutes) I went for a walk along the shore and I could feel my pores shouting *hallelujah!* at the fresh moist clean breeze.

I'm taking a break from the schoolwork right now. It's nine-thirty at night and raining and I have all the windows open (there are no screens on them. There don't seem to be any mosquitoes here. Can you dig that?) Anyhow, as I said, I'm sitting here listening to the soft rain. *The small rain down can rain* (impressive literary quote). I was going to pick up the phone and call you but then I remembered it's midnight or thereabouts where you are. Besides, if I did call you we'd gab until two in the morning, and I have to get this paper done tonight.

I called your friend James when I arrived and he helped me find a decent place to stay that's not far from the university (and not too expensive either). You'll think I bullied him into helping me but I swear I didn't. He was the one who suggested it, and insisted. Such a nice guy, and damn nice looking, too, which you didn't bother to mention. Just because you're a married old lady doesn't mean you're not allowed to notice these things. From what you told me about his work I was expecting some bearded, confrontational hippy type. Bigfoot with a Ph.D. But he's not like that at all, is he? In fact, he looks and acts like a holdover from the fifties, with those serious glasses and that haircut. I did have to laugh at the beat-up used van he drives. The previous owner had painted groovy designs on it, along with the word "Nir-Van-a" on the side door and James hadn't bothered repainting. You'd expect a certain kind of guy to be driving something like that. But he had no idea what my "Frodo Lives" button meant, and he hasn't even read *The Lord of the Rings!*

Another surprise: I showed up at his office one day, to take him to lunch as a thank you, and lo and behold he doesn't work in a rat's nest of paper stacked to the ceiling! The only academic I've ever met who can actually see the floor of his office. I don't know about this guy. He's so neat and tidy and meticulous with his stuff, and no girlfriend in sight. Kind of makes you wonder…

Yesterday afternoon he took me to Michael's tree. "Scotty" is a handsome fellow who still has a ways to go to be monarch of the forest. Or lord of the lawn, anyhow. As it was sunny and warm for a change we made a picnic of it. We sat on a blanket and ate smoked salmon and crackers and shared a bottle of white wine, and watched the ships and the sailboats in the bay. This has to be the most beautiful spot in the entire world for a city. You have to get out here and see it!

You know how I work. Once James had a couple of glasses of wine I started pressing him, in my subtle way, for life details. Seems he had a lady love, once. This was a long time ago, though, so don't scratch theory above just yet. He didn't say much about her and I got the feeling he's still hurting over that one. He did talk a lot about you, though. He thinks you're the cat's silk pajamas, my friend. The boys always did like you better, you scrawny little twerp.

Well, I've got to get back to work, but one more thing, something that James asked me to pass on to you. I hope you know what this means because I certainly don't. He said to tell you that the correct term for what most people call a "tidal wave" is a *tsunami*, that they are caused not by tides but by earthquakes on the ocean floor, and that no one who's been through one will ever forget it.

Is this some kind of coded secret message? What's up with you two?

Ever yours,
Nancy

P.S. Hugs and kisses to my adorable godchild.

P.P.S. Tell your bigshot husband he needs to tie on an apron and let you out on parole from baby jail for a while. Preferably to here!

P.P.P.S. "Baby jail" wasn't nice. More hugs and kisses to Michael! XOXOXOXO

New York USA
September 27 1977

Dear Nancy,

I'm not surprised to hear that the wild northwest hasn't quailed your spirit. Not that I think anything could. Thank you for the news about Michael's tree. Your picnic by the bay sounds lovely. I'm sitting here on a smoggy grey Manhattan afternoon and thinking unkind thoughts about you lounging in the sun. I enjoyed your description of James and his office, too, which made me laugh out loud. It's strange: I think of him a good friend, and yet in many ways I know so little about him.

Thanks also for passing on James's message about tidal waves. You can relay one to him from me: in keeping with the aquatic theme, did he know that salmon was at one time the major food source of Europe? It was once so plentiful that in the Middle Ages apprentices would have a clause put in their contracts stipulating that they would be served salmon only twice a week.

Don't tell James I saw this on PBS. I have a reputation to keep up as a keen, relentless newshound.

Secret messages? You have such a suspicious nature.

Hugs and kisses from Michael.
All my love,
Martha

Vancouver, Canada
October 10 1977

Dear Cuz,

James did not know that about salmon. He wondered where you had dug up such an interesting tidbit. Dear God the two of you need to get out more. I did not reveal that you gleaned your fish knowledge from TV, but I don't think he'll catch you on that, because he doesn't own an idiot box. Yes, I've been in the man's house. No, I did not force my way in, he invited me. His bachelor pad is not quite as neat as his office (theory taking a beating now) since he keeps all of his mementos from his various trips here and he hasn't gotten around to arranging them. It's a very small house to cram so much stuff in. James lives in North Vancouver, almost out of the city in a hillside neighborhood of old houses that are being torn down one by one to build mansions for the rich. His is one of the last – to be honest -- *shacks* in the area. But I can see why he loves it. Three steps out the back door and you're on a path up into the forest. It's gorgeous but kind of scary at the same time. Who knows what kind of creature could come out of those trees, human or otherwise.

    The inside of the house is even more quaint. When I first came in I tripped over the shrunken heads on the floor. Just kidding. No shrunken heads, but a lot of far-out stuff: shells and eggs and rocks with fossils in them and strange creepy-looking plants growing everywhere. He also keeps his camping and travel gear handy in case he has to fly out the door in search of some exciting new fungi he hasn't met yet. Sorry, that's not fair. He really is one of the coolest people I've ever known and you know I'm not easily impressed.

As always I tried to worm personal information out of him, but now that he's spent a little time with me he's gotten more cagey.

Case in point:

Me: This is a cool thing (picking up a small ceramic bowl).

JW: That was a gift.

Me: Oh, from who?

JW: A good friend.

Me: She has good taste. I mean, if she *is* a she.

JW: It's a lovely piece, isn't it? Have you heard of kintsugi?

Me: Is that your friend's name? Is she Chinese?

JW: (launching into full "answer man" mode) No, kintsugi is the Japanese art of mending broken pottery with lacquer and gold or silver, to make something even more beautiful than before. The idea is that you don't try to hide the damage, you make it part of the history of the object.

Me: Wow, that's far out. Did your friend do this herself?

JW: (as if he hasn't heard my question) I'm told it's an expression of things simply being what they are in this world. Everything changes, nothing remains the same. Stuff breaks. But even something broken is still valuable and filled with beauty. It apparently began with another Japanese art called ...

I could go on, and so can he, but I'm sure you get the idea.

Speaking of salmon, Jimbo (he hates me calling him that, hee hee!) took me to a salmon barbecue last night at a place called Spanish Banks, where I got to meet some of his tree-hugger friends. They built a big fire and set the salmon on cedar planks that they'd soaked beforehand so it wouldn't burn too quickly. The skin gets a bit charred on the underside but it actually adds to the flavor. One of the most delicious meals I've ever had, eating like a shipwreck survivor among the driftwood.

One of James's buddies is this *knockout handsome* Indian man named Clarence. He's from the same Coast Salish band as Chief Dan George, the Hollywood actor. He's good-looking enough to be a movie star too. Ooh Momma! Clarence told us stories that his grandfather had told him, about how things used to be in the old days, before the white man came along and messed everything up. Clarence said his grandfather told him, "When the white man first showed up, we had the land and they had the bibles. Now they have the land and we have the bibles." Then he laughed and winked at me. I actually blushed. Me! He has the most beautiful, deep, soft voice — okay, okay. Yes I was a little smitten. (I also keep thinking about how different the men are here from the New York variety. They're so easygoing here and not all uptight about their image. Not trying to impress me with their godlike maleness.)

(I also don't know why I'm using parentheses. Are these parts of the letter supposed to be whispered or something? Odd convention, isn't it. The thing is I'm enjoying all this letter-writing – for some reason it makes these stories even more fun to tell)

Anyhow back to the salmon cookout: the talk went all over the place, from favorite sports teams, to the space shuttle launch, to the history of North America and how native people have been treated. Or rather, mistreated. Someone said white society turns everything into just two things: money and garbage. I didn't know what to say to that. I thought I should be offended but James didn't seem to be so I just shut my yap and listened. I learned quite a lot, sister. It was enlightening, to say the least, for someone like me who grew up on John Wayne movies. Remember how my brothers, when they needed someone to be the Apaches in their games of cowboys and Indians, always picked me? Nobody else wanted to be the Indians because they always lost. Or maybe it was because I could make as much noise as a whole war party. Anyhow the talk got on to things that people had seen or heard tell of far and wide. I learned that there's a mysterious herd of wild horses in the Pryor Mountains of Montana, and the Crow people who live there say the herd is descended from the surviving horses of Custer's army. The battle of the Little Bighorn took place only a few miles away from where they roam now.

You see what's happening to me? I've only been here a month and I'm starting to turn into one of you gee-whiz fact-collectors! But seriously, I think I'm beginning to figure out where James gets his nuggets of fascinating-but-useless information: he listens to people. He's a great listener. And he'd have to be, to put up with

Yours truly,
Nancy

P.S. Groovy fact o' the week from James: he once took a stroll over hot coals. It was in a village in Guatemala, during a fire-walking ceremony. First he had to make sure the soles of his feet were brushed free of dirt and grass. Then he was told to step forcefully across the bed of coals without hesitating or slowing down (as if you'd want to stop and take in the scenery). He did as he was told and made it across the coals without any sensation of pain, and no burns or blisters in the slightest.

P.P.S. Still perplexed, but well-fed. Love to Michael. When are you coming out here???

New York, USA
November 8 1977

Dear Nancy,

It sounds like you're having an amazing time, and I'd love nothing more than to come for a visit, but things are difficult at the moment. Uncle Henry's condition has been getting worse, and Philip is really finding it tough to deal with. I know what you'd probably say about Philip's needs after what he put me through, but I just don't feel right about leaving right now. I hope you understand.

To make things even more complicated, we now have care of a cat that Uncle Henry bought a while back to keep him company, a lovely grey female that he named Magnificat. He can't look after the poor thing anymore, of course, but now she's gone and had a litter of kittens. So in the midst of everything else I'm running around trying to find homes for them. Not much luck.

Then yesterday morning I woke up and the kittens, that I'd put at the foot of the bed in a hamper, had crawled up in the night to get warm and were nestled in my hair, biting and sucking at my scalp for milk. As far as I know that qualifies as a previously unrecorded feline behavior.

All the best,
Martha

Vancouver, Canada
December 1 1977

Dear Martha,

Nancy has told me what's been happening in your life at present. I'm sorry to hear that things are not going well for Philip's uncle.

Your story of the kittens was one I had never heard before. Whether wild cats would behave similarly is a question that may be a long time finding an answer. The only wild felines in this part of the world are cougars, who are sometimes found surprisingly close to the city. There was a bizarre incident here a couple of years back. All of the small dogs in a neighbourhood near the edge of town began to disappear. Eventually a cougar was discovered living in a scraped-out den under a house trailer. She had a litter of cubs and was feeding them with the local pets.

Nancy has been quite a trooper. I've hauled her all around Stanley Park and on a few hikes further afield, and so far she hasn't complained that I'm boring her to death with tales of nurse logs and the miracle of mycorrhizae. Our last outing was in Clarence's boat up along the coast north of here. He and his brothers take people eagle-watching for a living. On this trip the weather came up all of a sudden, as it does, and things got quite choppy for a while, but Nancy seemed to be enjoying herself. Neither of us got seasick, at any rate, and she had us all laughing with her jokes and goofing off. We spotted a huge eagle's nest at the top of a towering Douglas fir and I told Nancy that the nest probably weighed close to two tons.

Her response: "Holy f--k!"

She swears like a sailor but she's full of surprises, isn't she? I get the feeling she's read nearly everything, and she can recite entire long poems from memory. Thanks to her I've discovered the writings of Emerson and Whitman and Henry David Thoreau (ashamed to say I never got around to *Walden* until now). Their books convey ideas and feelings that I know very well but never had the language to express.

Here's a quote from Emerson I particularly like:
"All the thoughts of a turtle are turtle."

Your friend,
James

Vancouver, Canada
January 9 1978

Om mane padme hum...

Hello Cuz, it's me, the nature goddess.

We just talked on the phone and here I am writing. I've definitely caught the epistolary bug from you and James. I like the fact that you don't call each other, you just write. It's so old-fashioned, but knowing you and having met him I can understand that's how it should be. Plus it's a hell of a lot cheaper than long distance.

Scratch that last paragraph. The truth is I'm writing because I'm afraid to say this right to you. Yes, ME, afraid. And no I haven't been drinking. This isn't an "e-pissed-olary" document (yeah, *groan*). Well, maybe it is, just a little. A couple glasses of prosecco worth.

Anyhow here goes, the deep dark secret that's making me blush like a schoolgirl right this minute: James. Yes I know he's absolutely not my type. But maybe that's just it. Maybe I've finally had enough of my "type." The exciting, dangerous guy who turns out to be, surprise, surprise, a selfish arsehole.

James and I have been to a couple of movies together, we've walked along the beach, we've hugged goodnight like good buddies. That's it. It's so innocent I can't quite believe it's me in this picture. Wow, I have a crush on this man. A *crush.* God! That's something I haven't had for a guy since ninth grade. You know my usual method - frontal assault, take no prisoners. But when I'm around him I get all light-headed and bubbly. I get the proverbial butterflies. I turn into a *girl!!!*

The butterflies would be Monarchs, I think. Did you know that a pair of mating monarchs will remain "in the position" for up to 16 hours? 16 hours! If there's such a thing as reincarnation, I know what I want to come back as. Hee! I swear I'm not drunk right now. At least not on booze.

One thing I don't know is how James feels about me. He's been stressed out the last couple of years with environmental battles and problems at the university, and his method of dealing with it all is to dig himself a foxhole in a pile of papers. He's not an outwardly emotional person at the best of times, except when he's talking about trees or endangered species. Even about the tree-hugging activities I've discovered he hasn't told me everything. Do you remember me mentioning Clarence, the hunky guy with the great voice at the beach cookout? (Already taken, by the way, sigh.) Clarence has filled me in on the sorts of things James has been up to. Last summer for example James went out on one of those Greenpeace expeditions, where they try to get between the whaling ships and the whales. And this summer he was involved in some sort of protest on an island north of here where logging has been clearing away an old-growth forest. There were people chaining themselves to bulldozers and things like that and James was right in the thick of it and got hauled off by the cops with the rest of the protestors (James had described it to me as if he'd just witnessed the whole thing and wasn't actually involved).

Clarence also told me that James has dated women from time to time but it never lasts long. His last relationship ended only a few months before I got here. Lucky for me. Ha ha. Clarence says the woman, whoever she was, complained to him once that James is a "permanent bachelor." Maybe she cracked that ceramic bowl over his head and then felt bad and got it kintsugied for him.

I'm in a bad way, cuz. I remember how you looked when you first started dating Philip. Lit up like a Christmas tree. All those clichés about how the world looks different blah blah blah. But it really does. Or maybe what happens is that you *see* differently. You become a person who sees in another way. That doesn't always happen of course. I've been with guys who knocked my socks off, literally, and there wasn't that feeling of transformation if that's the right word for it. Jesus, listen to me. I'm so glad I chose to write this instead of picking up the phone again. I may still tear this letter up before I get to the yours truly part.

The other night James and I went for a walk along the river. That's all we did – walked and talked, our breath coming out in clouds in the damp freezing night air. I thought *I should be bored as hell with this*, but I wasn't. I was happy. This was all I needed.

Now isn't that the most amazing little facteroonie you've ever heard?

Lots of the "ell" word, and hugs and kisses to the world's sweetest little boy!

Ever the fool,

Nancy

P.S. Here's the *really* embarrassing part. I'm going to ask you to break confidence: since I've been here has there been anything in James's letters that might give a bad girl hope?

P.P.S. Don't worry. I've got a part-time job in a bookstore near campus. It doesn't pay much but I love the place (you wouldn't believe the ranting nutcases that come in here. It's almost like home). And with the inheritance from my dad I'm doing okay.

P.P.P.S. *Get out here, girl!*

From Martha Geddes' diary
Jan 27 1978

Another day without much progress on the new article. Tired of it really. There's probably a good reason why most of what the body does is meant to go unnoticed. Otherwise we'd spend all our time obsessing with things that runs just fine on their own. Better to worry only about the stuff that isn't working. Which appears to be what I'm doing with the article and with the rest of my life. Philip is out late again tonight.

Today Michael put a new sentence together, one that probably no one's ever said before. I was sitting at my desk not writing, Michael was playing with his toys on the floor beside me, and a cockroach crawled out of my typewriter keyboard. I yelled – scared Michael pretty good and impressed the cockroach, too, I think. It scuttled off the side of the typewriter and promptly vanished.

I told Michael what happened and he wanted to see the cockroach. He peered into the depths of the keyboard and then he looked at me and said, "Write more bugs, Mommy."

That might be a good idea, really. An article on this ubiquitous insect that we Manhattanites have resigned ourselves to cohabiting with. A kind of celebrity profile of the roach: "one of New York's most notorious but shy and least-understood denizens." Something to think about.

I should write back to Nancy. Told myself I haven't had time, but really I've been putting it off. Why is this so difficult? I don't have any claim on JW. But something about this just doesn't feel right. Still, what did I think was going to happen when I made the introductions between them? Well, probably not this.

New York, USA
January 27 1978

Dear Nancy,

Sorry it's taken me so long to write back. I think for the first time in a long time you managed to shock me. It never crossed my mind you'd be attracted to someone like James. On the one hand, I think I can understand how you feel. James is like a little boy in the way he's fascinated by the things most of us take for granted. He hasn't lost the openness to wonder that children have, and that's a very attractive quality.

Still, I really think you should be careful. Take the time to figure out if this is, as you said yourself, just a crush, or something deeper. At the least I think you're right not to rush the man. He's someone who can roam a cold, rainy forest for hours, waiting for a glimpse of some rare bird. You've got to be patient, too.

Love,
Martha

Vancouver, Canada
February 4 1978

Dear Cuz,

Have to say your letter bummed me out a bit. When did you become my prim old auntie? But you're right, you're right. As usual, dammit. I guess I was hoping for an adolescent gasp and shriek from my favorite cousin and confidante, followed by a rousing "go get 'im, girl!" I miss those sleep-overs we used to have as teenagers, giggling about the cute boys at school and playing our Beatles records over and over until your dad roared at us to shut that damn long-haired music off and go to sleep. Long-haired music, heh. I miss your pop.

Dramatic sigh! I wish you were here to get me laughing about this whole sorry mess. In your last letter I think you got closer to the heart of JW than I have, even though I've spent so much time with him lately. If this is only a passing infatuation I could be ruining a great friendship. And God knows you've seen the awful results of my spontaneity in the past (I still may have to have you assassinated one day for what you've witnessed). In one way it's a good thing I haven't seen much of James lately—he's been totally caught up in the fight over that island. This more than anything, I suspect, has kept me from making an utter and complete ass of myself. Yet again. Which I may yet do. Keep ya posted.

Love, and lots of kisses for Michael,
Nancy

Vancouver, Canada
March 7 1978

Dear Martha,

I am writing to let you know that Persephone Island's fate
has been decided.

I'm sitting on my front porch writing this letter. It's
early morning, and far from this quiet city street the power
saws are starting to cut into the ancient trees, a sound that's
never been heard in that forest before. I swear I can almost
feel the crack and shudder of those toppling giants from
here. But I'm taking your advice and sitting out the dance
for a while. I got a leave of absence for a year. Time to go
traveling again.

The truth is I feel pretty much used up. I have no
doubt Nancy is one of the reasons I haven't burnt out
completely. All that excess energy of hers. I think I've been
recharging myself with it somehow. When we got the news
about Persephone Island, Nancy suggested that if I was
looking for some peace I should visit the Himalayas. She
went there when she was barely out of high school, with
her pot-smoking musician boyfriend. Quite a story. I
especially liked the part where he decided that from now
on she would be known as Dharma Child and he would
answer to Shining Mandala. Anyhow, she has a point about
getting out of here for a while.

All the best,
James

New York, USA
March 15 1978

Dear James,

I am truly sorry to hear about Persephone Island. It must be a terrible disappointment for you, and a great loss. I think your plan to take some time off is a sensible one.

I'm not surprised, that Nancy's helped you get through these tough times. Over the years I've always relied on her to cheer me up or to kick my rear into gear when it needed kicking. And yes, I know the stories of her Great Himalayan Trek with Stephen the Transcendent One. Who was so enlightened he didn't think twice about abandoning her in some remote village while he went off to search for Beauty and Truth. With a pretty Australian girl, if I remember correctly. I don't think Nancy regretted that trip, though. It helped her find her own inner resources. If she believes a trip there will do you good, I'm sure she's right.

I'm writing an exposé on the cockroach. A fascinating subject. Their capacity for survival is legendary. They can go for weeks without food or water. Their pressure-sensitive body hairs can alert them to the tiniest sounds, never mind the descending swish of a rolled-up newspaper. The fossil record shows they've remained relatively unchanged in 300 million years. Why mess with success?

The female of some species, I've learned, mates once and is pregnant for the rest of her life. I wonder if the

Catholic Church knows about this. Newborn roaches come out of the egg case colorless but all ready and raring to skitter off. The other day at the Museum of Natural History I got to examine a Madeira cockroach under a microscope. I squinted into the eyepiece, prepared to flinch back in disgust, but not prepared for what I did find — beauty. A creature more intricate and complex than I had ever guessed at. The shell of its body is shiny with a waxlike secretion that renders it waterproof. It has two antenna-like feelers on its head, the maxillary papillae, for sampling food before it is eaten, which helps the roach avoid poison. The design of its jaw alone is a marvel. I don't think Kafka bothered to look through a microscope when he dreamt up poor Gregor Samsa.

Speaking of insects, the gardening bug has truly bitten me — on these wet, grey spring days I can't wait for an opportunity to visit my little plot of land and dig my fingers into the cold, awakening earth. Even early in the morning there are always one or two others here, working quietly in their own patches. Sometimes we chat, sometimes nothing is said. We know why we're here, there's no need to make polite noises. I see an elderly Japanese couple here often. The woman brought over a bucket of what looked and smelled like mulched fish, and with smiles and nods showed me to gently fold and turn the earth to work the stuff in. I asked her what it was but her English is limited to a few basic phrases. Instead she took my hand, placed it on the earth we had just turned and patted it softly, which said as clearly as words that we were feeding the soil with good things.

When we're done, Michael and I walk home with muddy boots and dirty hands. It always feels like we've been away, in another country, for a long time.

Take care, James. Write to me, and come home safe and sound.

Wishing you all the best,
Martha

Vancouver, Canada
April 19 1978

Dear Cuz,

Please pass on to Philip my deepest sympathies about
Uncle Henry. I only met him the one time at your wedding
but I know he was a kind and generous man. A real old-
style gentleman. It was clear you and Philip thought the
world of him.

The school term is almost over and if you'd like me to
come home and stay with you for a while just say the word.
I suppose I would only be in your way, but just let me
know. Okay? I'd like to see my godson again anyway. It's
been far too long.

I suppose this isn't the best time for it but I wanted to
let you know that in the end I didn't take your advice about
James. I was my old impatient self and the results were ...
strange.

James has decided to go to Nepal this summer, after
I'd bugged him about it enough. But when he told me this
the other day it suddenly hit me he was going to be gone
for a long time. And I suppose I was thinking about
Stephen, too. How he found his cosmic soulmate over
there and left me hurtin' like a gal in a country song. So I
panicked. I got it into my head that if I didn't make my
feelings clear before James left I might not get a chance
afterward.

Well, a few evenings ago I went for broke. With
cunning aforethought I brought over a bottle of wine to

enhance the mood (or dull the fear), and we shared it and got a little tipsy, and yeah, okay, I threw myself at the guy. James didn't exactly turn me down, but before things got too steamy we both called a halt. I know how dopey this is gonna sound but I felt like some kind of a telepathic connection between us that said this was wrong, this was not how things were supposed to be. Like a psychic splash of cold water. Both of us were suddenly embarrassed. James started apologizing and I told him there was nothing to apologize for, it was my mistake, and so on, and then I got the heck out of there.

I spent a sleepless night reliving my stupidity in every glorious detail and thinking *great, now you've lost a friend. Way to go, moron.* But the next morning James called me and we went out for dinner and we had a really good time. As friends. Honest! With anyone else that would have been impossible. We talked about Nepal and the Himalayas and as I sat there blathering away about what he needed to bring on his trip and what to watch out for, etc etc, it dawned on me that I was cured. Of my crush, I mean. As much as it irritates me to admit it, you were right. *Don't go rushing in,* you said, and now I can hear saying *I told you so.* But it's okay. It's all good. In fact I think it was for the best to get all that out of my system. I know, I sound so horribly, unnaturally *mature.* Don't worry, it won't last.

After dinner we went for a walk and James told me he needed to explain something about what had happened the other night. I insisted he didn't need to explain anything but of course I was hanging on his every word. I thought I was finally going to get some answers to the riddle of James Wheeler.

He told me that some time ago he met the woman he was sure he was meant to be with in this life. He'd never felt that absolute certainty before and he'd never imagined that he would, but there was no denying it. The trouble is, for some reason they can't be together. I'm guessing she must be the long-lost love he hinted at the day we went to see the tree. You should have seen his face, Martha, when he was talking about her. I asked him if the woman still felt the same way and he said that when they first met he was sure of it, but then he found out he was wrong. She has her own life, one he doesn't share.

Anyhow since this woman turned his life upside down he hasn't been able to commit himself to anyone else. He told me that his last romantic relationship hadn't worked out for that reason, the one that ended not long before I arrived. He said he valued our friendship and didn't want the same thing to happen to us. Now as you know I've heard a line or two in my time, but I believe him. I really do. He isn't just trying to soften the blow with a nice story.

"So I guess I'm a confirmed bachelor," he said.

"For God's sake, you sound like a musty old fart," I shouted at him, and we both laughed.

"No, I'm just a *bachelor*," he said again, with a funny kind of emphasis on the word. What was he getting at? I couldn't figure it out.

So here we are, and this is all just so weird. The old me would be in hiding now, eating entire pints of chocolate ice cream at one sitting and calling you three times a night to bawl and curse the guy's name. But I'm okay. Things really have turned out for the best. I just don't get this guy, in both senses of the word. Hah. He remains a riddle wrapped in an enigma inside one nice hunk of manhood. And next month off he goes to Nepal where he'll probably meet a smoldering Himalayan beauty who'll capture his soul and they'll live in a mountain hut and have ten kids and then he'll ascend to the plane of cosmic all-knowingness and we'll never hear from him again. The jerk.

Can't say I'm deliriously happy, but at least that *romance* baloney is over and done with.

Dazed and confused and wish you were here,
Nancy

P.S. Little-known fact: the female of the species sometimes acts like a complete fool.

New York, USA
April 24 1978

Dear Nancy,

I'm glad to hear that everything turned out for the best, as you say, and that you and James are still good friends. I'm not saying "I told you so." Did I ever say that? I hope not.

Philip asked me to thank you for the kind words about Uncle Henry. He is handling this quite well, really, but of course I would love to have you come home and stay with us for a while. No reason required. I'll split that pint of chocolate ice cream with you, whether either of us need it or not.

Please give my best wishes and a *bon voyage* to James. There may be smoldering Himalayan beauties over there, but James with kids? I just don't see it.

Love,
Martha

Chitwan Wilderness Preserve, Nepal
June 21 1978

Dear Martha,

I've spent three weeks trekking in the Himalayas and now I'm exploring a region known as the Terai, a lowland along the southwestern edge of Nepal that forms part of the Gangetic plain. Nature reserves have been set up here in recent years to deal with poaching of rare animals and the destruction of the forest for fuel and farmland. In the early part of the century, so I've been told, this area was thick malarial jungle that kept the British barbarians out of the territory of the Nepalese kings. A kind of green, living Great Wall.

When I first arrived in this area, I hired an elephant and driver at the Gaida Wilderness Camp. The driver's name was Adesh and the elephant's was Bhai, which means brother. It was a magical way to travel. I'd be looking around at the sights and then suddenly I'd remember I was sitting on the back of a living thing and be shocked and amazed all over again that this massive creature was allowing me to use it as a conveyance. I got to thinking, what must it *feel* like to be an elephant? To be this size, to have an elephant's senses and way of seeing the world? What does an elephant think of *us*? They're said to be sensitive, intuitive creatures underneath that thick hide.

As incredible as the experience was, I soon realized that traveling so high off the ground was keeping me too far above the plants and flowers. So after a couple days I paid Adesh the full amount I would have owed him and said farewell to him and to Bhai, who seemed completely unmoved about us parting ways. Then I hoisted my pack and set off hiking on my own.

The plant life here is profuse and all new to me. There are hundreds of species of orchids alone.

What would this letter be without a little-known fact? The upper Ganges is home to a species of beaked freshwater dolphin called the susu, also known as the blind dolphin. Because of its poor eyesight it swims on its side under the water, keeping one flipper trailing in the riverbed.

There is a tradition that the God Krishna loved this land and used to wander these fields and forests in the evening, when the setting sun turned everything to gold just for love of him. Of course that's just a myth, but it is peaceful here.

With best regards,
James

Katmandu, Nepal
June 29 1978

Dear Martha,

Greetings from Bir Hospital in Katmandu. On the enclosed map I circled a spot in the lower right hand corner. That's roughly where the accident happened, in the Karnali River gorge of Bardia National Park. I was off the beaten track, as usual, and surprised some poachers cutting up a rhino carcass. Or I should say we surprised each other. I'd been walking along the gorge in the rain and heard a couple of shots in the distance. Probably should've gone to find Norbu Yunten, the park ranger who'd taken me into the park earlier in the day and whose station wasn't far away from where I was exploring. But I didn't. Decided to have a look for myself first. Mistake.

I was pushing through some dense vegetation and then suddenly there they were, three of them in a clearing with the dead rhino, hacking off the poor thing's horns with machetes. I saw them, they saw me, and the chase was on. Without thinking I headed back in the direction of the gorge, since that was going to be my reference point for finding my way back to Norbu's station at the end of the day. Of course with my attention focused on what was behind me I wasn't paying much attention to what was in front of me and I ran right off the edge of the gorge into thin air. The poachers declined to follow. Or maybe they were satisfied the seven hundred foot drop had taken care of me. Anyhow I lay on a mossy rock ledge for about five hours, much of it thankfully unconscious, before Norbu Yunten and another ranger found me. They'd heard the shots too and had been out looking for the poachers, who were long gone by then. Fortunately the rangers stumbled upon me before heading home for the day. I had a lot of time to study the phenomenon of pain, at any rate. With two cracked ribs, a broken ankle, and a concussion I consider myself pretty lucky.

The ankle was in a bad way. They had to do surgery, so it will be a while before I get home. Still it's not all terrible. Norbu has been very kind. He couldn't stay with me in Katmandu but his brother's family lives here and he let them know about me. They've been visiting and bringing me delicious home-cooked meals. None of them speak English so they sit around my bed while I eat and we smile and nod at each other a lot.

Regards,
James

P.S. Norbu told me that in 1939 the last major British hunting party killed 100 tigers here on one expedition, about as many as are left in the entire park today.

New York, USA
July 15 1978

Dear James,

Your letter with the map arrived yesterday. As you know, Nancy has been keeping me informed pretty much daily about your return home and your recovery, so the news in the postcard didn't come as a shock, although the depth of the gorge did. It's terrible to think what it must have been like for you, lying there all that time, not knowing if you would ever be found. I'm just glad you didn't end up like that poor rhino. And you're also lucky one of those hundred remaining tigers didn't cross your path.

I think you'll like the enclosed clipping.

With my best wishes for a speedy recovery,
Martha

Zoo tiger introduced into the wild
Dudhawa, India

A tiger born in the Twycross Zoo in Leicestershire, England, has been introduced into a forest preserve in northern India, in the hopes of proving that artificial restocking can help save this endangered species.

Arjan "Billy" Singh, well-known here as the father of big-cat conservation, brought the female cub, Tara the tigress, to his farm near Dudhawa National Park in 1976, where she lived until Singh let her loose in the park earlier this year. Tara is known to have some Siberian Tiger ancestry, which has led critics to argue that Singh is tampering with the purity of the native gene pool. Singh counters that this genetic diversity is key to the survival of the tiger, since the low number of animals remaining leads to fatal interbreeding.

"Our own lives depend on the biodiversity of the environment," Singh said in an interview. "At the centre of this truth are the large mammals, like the tiger. If the tiger goes, we go."

Vancouver, Canada
July 31 1978

Dear Martha,

Thank you for your concern, it means more to me than I can express. And I'm grateful for the heartening story of Tara, which was sorely needed. I've been so doped up on painkillers I feel like I've been cramming all the "trips" I missed out on during my college years into the last few weeks. I've been out of sorts and lethargic, too. Very strange for me. Nancy has been my indispensable nurse/cook/therapist/coach. And a great rear-kicker. When she met me at the airport she said, "I warned you not to go there," and we had a good laugh. These days she comes over without fail every morning and practically has to boot me out of bed, otherwise I'd lie there staring at the wall. I've read about soldiers returning from the Vietnam war who fall into this kind of mood. A kind of lingering shell-shock. Maybe something like that can happen to a person after an accident. I don't know, it's not a feeling I've ever been familiar with. Guess I've been lucky that way.

Your friend,
James

P.S. Haven't taken a measurement of Michael's tree yet this summer, for obvious reasons. I'll get back to you about that as soon as I can.

In the meantime, here is a sketch for Michael, from my journal, of an animal that is a great tree-climber: the Malayan binturong, a sad-faced, tree-dwelling carnivore related to the mongoose. I met this interesting fellow on my last trip to Southeast Asia, a few years ago.

The binturong's feet can rotate 180 degrees, enabling it to climb down trees head first. They apparently have a powerful scent gland under the tail. I swear that the one I saw gave off an aroma a lot like buttered popcorn (or maybe I was still experiencing nature as a kid in a theatre watching *White Wilderness*). I sat motionless for over an hour waiting for him to come down out of the leaves so I could get a good look at him. Then I discovered I'd forgotten to put film in the camera. It was a truly tropical wet, drizzly day, and I caught a nasty cold, but he was worth it.

New York, USA
August 10 1978

Dear James,

I appreciate the progress reports on the tree, but Nancy and I don't want you climbing up on a ladder, do you hear? Just let Scotty grow for a season, and then it will surprise us even more next year.

Thank you for the binturong. Michael was impressed, and wanted to go to the zoo to see if they had any. They did not, but we had a great time nonetheless. We were delighted in particular by the baby giraffe, playing hide-and-seek around its mothers legs. We discovered from reading a placard that a giraffe's tongue is so long it can clean its own ears with it. When I explained this to Michael, he spent the next ten minutes trying to perform the same feat, which earned us some funny looks from people walking by.

At the gift shop I bought Michael a little ark of toy animals, and he's playing with them on my office floor as I write this. He has them arranged in a peaceable circle and he is busy talking in all their voices.

Warm regards,
Martha

Vancouver, Canada
September 29 1978

Dear Cuz,

You'll be glad to know that James's condition continues to improve. He's back at work now and insists he's doing fine, but I'm not so sure. Physically he's healing just fine, more quickly than expected actually, but something happened to him in Nepal, other than the accident I mean. And by the way it really bugs me that he insists on calling it an "accident." Three machete-wielding bad guys chasing you through the jungle is not an accident, it's attempted murder. Anyhow James has never told me what's wrong but it's obvious he's not the same exasperating lovable Jimbo he was before this happened. Something hit him hard, and I don't mean the bottom of that gorge he fell into. That was just the physical trauma. The truth is I haven't seen him a lot the past while and when we run into each other I get the feeling he'd rather I just left him alone. I'm not the only one who's noticed, either. Clarence says the same thing about his friend and he's known him a lot longer than I have. When Clarence and I do get together with James, which almost never happens anymore, it's difficult to get a laugh or even a smile out of him. Not that he was exactly Charlie Chuckles before but there's this gloom over him now. One of the few things that cheers him up is a letter from you.

Here's what I think, for what it's worth (I'm a psychotherapist now, okay?) I know his mother died when he was quite young but I don't know if he's ever faced the fact of his own mortality. It seems to me that someone who likes to root around in rainforests sees life as something eternal, with all that green stuff springing up, blooming, rioting. New things growing on dead things. Life as an endless cycle, renewing itself again and again. You'd get used to that, I think. Maybe you'd forget that something has to die before something else can live. Maybe that day James spent at the bottom of a gorge with a broken ankle showed him that the cycle will go on without him. He's not immortal.

I don't know, maybe I'm way off track, but it's not hard to see that something just isn't right.

I've been hinting in my subtle way he should come with me to New York for a visit but so far he hasn't taken the bait. He cancelled a couple of trips he was supposed to go on this season and I really think that what he needs is to get out of here for a while. And if anybody can cheer him up it would be you. I'll keep working on the New York idea and let you know if I have any success.

Love,
Nancy

New York, USA
October 11 1978

Dear James,

Nancy tells me you are back at work and recovering from your injuries. I'm so glad to hear it.

As you know, it's a dream of mine to visit China some day, and so over the years I have made it a point to learn as much as I can about that country. Recently I discovered that one of the most common trees in New York is originally from China: the ginkgo. The old Japanese couple I garden with told me this. It turns out they know more English than they let on at first. Their names are Kenji and Hikari Kaneshiro. They came to the States in the early fifties with their two children, who are grown up now.

Once you start looking, you see ginkgo trees all over New York. I had never paid them much attention before, but they really are lovely. The leaves turn so quickly. One day they are green and the next they're yellow and falling to the ground in droves.

The ginkgo was once neglected, perhaps because the fruit of the female tree gives off such an unpleasant odor as it rots. The species was saved from extinction in its native China by Buddhist monks, who started to cultivate the wild tree in their monasteries. They called the leaves "Buddha's fingernails."

It's strange to think of this tree's journey: thriving for millions of years, outlasting catastrophic climate change, then almost dying out, and now gracing the streets of a city so far from its home. There are trees here that were planted in the eighteenth century, I've been told, and they seem to do just fine in the smoggy city air.

It stands to reason that a tree this old would have many legends associated with it. Thanks to the Kaneshiros, I took part in a Japanese tea ceremony the other day, for a piece I'm doing on the Brooklyn Botanic Garden (I find I'm being classified as a "nature writer" more and more these days, which is fine). Hikari, it turns out, is a tea ceremony expert who's often called in by the Garden to make sure everything goes according to ritual and tradition. While we were there Kenji told me the story of a teahouse in Kyoto that was saved by a ginkgo tree. In the 1600's, a fire swept through the city and most of its buildings were destroyed. The teahouse survived, however, because of the ginkgo tree under which it sheltered. The snow held by the tree's large, fan-shaped leaves melted in the heat and dripped on the teahouse roof, keeping it damp so that sparks from the surrounding fire could not take hold.

Your friend,
Martha

New York, USA
January 12 1979

Dear James,

Best wishes to you for the new year. I hope you are well.

The holiday season has just ended, there's snow on the frozen ground, but I already find myself thinking about the garden. It's all there in my mind: the wet green leaves, the flowers, the busy drone of the bees. I even went to have a look the other day. It was mid-morning when I set out, but it felt like twilight. Snow had been falling all night. The streets were like white tunnels and the cars crept quietly past as if they were half-asleep and wandering. When I reached the garden it was, of course, buried under a blanket of white. I unlocked the gate and went in anyway. In the undisturbed snow I found only the tracks of a bird. It had touched down there, perhaps, like me, out of a habit learned in another season, walked around for a bit, and taken off again.

Something that's been growing all winter is Michael's vocabulary. And his imagination. Philip was working over the holidays, and so Michael and I went out to my mother's place. On Christmas Eve we went outside to decorate the pine tree in the yard. Mom opened the cellar hatch to look for an extension cord, and Michael peered down the stairs and informed us that the subway was down there. And then he just plunked himself down there and sat looking intently into the dark of the cellar. Mom asked him if something was wrong, if he wanted to go home and he said no. He told us that if there was a subway here, that meant Daddy could come for dinner.

My Mom says this proves we don't get out of the city enough, but even if that's the case it's clear that Michael appreciates nature. He's fascinated by animals. That trip we took to the zoo last summer to look for a binturong really made an impact on him. He is drawing a lot now, too, and I can watch the change in his interests and his way of seeing the world in his artwork. Enclosed is one of his latest productions. The creature in the tree is indeed a binturong, based on the drawing you sent us. Believe it or not, the stick figure at the bottom of the page is you. I told Michael about how you explore the forests all by yourself and how sometimes you run into amazing creatures like the binturong, and he was so impressed he went right to his crayons and drew the scene. I may be guilty of embellishing the story a little, but anyhow it seems Michael now thinks of you as a cross between Max from *Where the Wild Things Are,* and Spider-man. In other words, you have a fan. And I didn't even tell him stories about you running off the edges of cliffs or climbing trees in a windstorm. I don't want him getting any ideas.

Warm regards,
Martha

Vancouver, Canada
March 3 1979

Dear Martha,

I apologize for the long delay in sending Michael my thanks for his drawing. I've never had a fan before. When he and I finally meet I hope he won't be too disappointed.

Nancy may have told you that I haven't been myself for some time. I think I'm finally coming back around. I didn't tell her about everything that happened to me in Nepal, because I didn't want to worry her.

It started in the hospital in Katmandu. When they knocked me out to put the screws in my ankle, I didn't go under. I was still conscious of what was going on in the operating room, or so it seemed. I could still hear the doctors speaking to one another and I could see what was going on in the room. I wanted to tell them I wasn't unconscious yet, but I couldn't make my voice work. Then things got even weirder. It felt as if something I hadn't really known to exist before by itself was leaving my body. I didn't have a name for it then but now I want to call it *awareness*. Just awareness, by itself, without the body or the usual mental chatter tagging along. Usually we feel that we're aware of things from inside our bodies, with our senses, and we don't give it a second thought. We never say to ourselves "This is me, these are my ears, aware of the sound of those birds chirping." It's just how we experience things and we don't imagine it could be any different. But there I was, or something was, floating up to a corner of the room and seeing my body lying there on the table as if it was someone else's body. Hey, I know him. That's James Wheeler. Poor guy, that's a nasty break.

It wasn't frightening, at least at first. Floating around as a disembodied awareness felt perfectly natural. I could zoom in, so to speak, on anything in the room that took my interest. There was a clock on a wall and I watched the minute hand advancing for a while. It seemed a funny way to measure time. Then I saw a little black beetle crawling along the ceiling tiles and it seemed even funnier that this operating room wasn't sterile like it was supposed to be. After a while it occurred to me to find out if this floating awareness could go even further. I concentrated on doing that—focusing my "vision" to see through the walls. And I started to. My gaze expanded, like a sphere, outside the hospital to the streets of the city, and even up into the hills around it. But at the same time it was like I was looking *into* things, as if my gaze was also going deeper, zooming in on smaller details, like a microscope. And all of it was crystal clear. I could see—I could hear and smell and taste and feel—everything. People, animals, a raindrop on a rhododendron leaf at the edge of the forest. *Everything*.

That's when the terror began.

As a scientist I had always felt there was some hidden significance in the fact that the "poles" of the vast and of the small in our universe are both inaccessible to us. Looking up, we can see no end to the cosmos, which observation tells us is expanding at an accelerating rate and growing ever more vast with each moment. We don't know how large our universe is, or will come to be. And looking within, we can't see or really measure the size of the tiniest components of matter, like the electrons which are apparently real only part of the time if quantum physics is to be believed, and the even smaller sub-subatomic particles that make up protons. We call them quarks but it's just a word. No one knows for certain what these things really are, or even *if* they are.

In that moment in the operating room, I felt as if with a little more effort I would be able to reach and know both poles, like an explorer who was somehow able to stand at both the North and the South Pole of the planet at the same time. I would see to the heart of the impossibly large and the vanishingly small. But more than that, there would be no *me* anymore.

It was beyond terrifying, really. I knew if I went there it would annihilate the person I had always been, but I couldn't stop myself. Nothing could stop this. And yet that body on the operating table was still me, as detached as I was. That James Wheeler still mattered to me. The people he loved and cared about, the things he still wished to do in life … those were still precious to him, and to me. But I couldn't tear myself away from what was about to happen. I wanted to know, to see, to *be* everything. And that everything was so close.

But at the same time something was holding me back, some other force. And now it was contracting again, my sphere of vision. The seeing was shrinking fast, back into the room, to me above the table, getting closer again to my body. The force *was* my body. Part of me fought against the pull, and part of me simply surrendered to it, accepted it.

Then I woke up back in my body, groggy and thirsty and blinking in the recovery room lights. The nurse told me it was two hours later and the operation was over. I was myself again, and more or less sane. The poles of the large and the small as impossibly far from me as they'd always been.

But it stayed with me longer than I expected, that vision. I sank into a gloom I couldn't shake off. I disconnected from everyone, from life, from myself. For a moment I'd glimpsed a larger, more meaningful world and now I was shut out of it.

Anyhow, Michael's drawing reminded me that it has been far too long since I took my own advice and looked for some small miracle right under my feet. So I did just that. I went for a long walk. I mean a really long walk. I grabbed a knapsack, some bottled water, some fruit and a couple of carrots, and just headed out the door and kept on going. No destination in mind, other than the thought that I would take a different direction than I'm usually inclined to, which meant I headed for the city instead of up into the hills.

The leg was a bit stiff at first but it warmed up pretty quickly. I walked all the way through North Vancouver and across the Lion's Gate Bridge, then into the downtown core, an area I usually avoid. So crowded and noisy and full of, well, unhappiness. I sat with the bums on the steps of the public library and ate my lunch. One of them came over and sat down beside me and started talking. First he asked me for money and I gave him a few dollars. He didn't go away, though. He stayed put and introduced himself as

Jerry. Said he was going to buy a bus ticket to go visit his mom in Winnipeg.

"This isn't your hometown?" I asked him.

"Naw, lived all over," he said. "Drove an oilfield supply truck to and from the tar sands for years. You know Fort McMurray?"

"I know of it. Never been there."

"Never drove the highway from Edmonton to the sands? The sixty-three?"

"No, I never have."

"Man, you haven't lived 'til you drive the highway of death. 'Specially in winter. I drove it nearly every day. The trees, man. All those trees. Gave me the creeps."

"The trees…?"

"Nothing for miles but f—ing trees, you know? Spruce, pine, fir. The dark trees you can't see through. I had like what they call a phobia, right? Scared the truck was gonna break down somewhere out there, miles from anywhere, in the dark, and then it'd just be me and the entire f—ing boreal. And sure as s—t one time it finally happened. Truck dies. Dead of goddamn winter, after sundown, north of Wandering River. You been there? No, right, you said you never been there. Sorry, I forgot. Mind's pretty much burnt up these days."

"What happened when you broke down?"

"That was the year I really got into the juice heavy. Knew I had a problem but I wasn't doing anything about it. Just drinking and tearing up the house like a demon. Old lady took our kid and moved out. I promised to quit. So she came back. And I started drinking all over again."

"So that night your truck broke down…"

141

"Yeah I was getting to that. I was gonna get on the radio and then wait in the cab until somebody come along to help. But I didn't do that. It was time, you know? To do something. For my kid. My baby girl. She was the one thing I did right. The one thing that meant I wasn't a complete f—k-up. So I tell myself *if you don't have the balls to quit then you might as well end it right now. Do it, f—khead. Take a long walk and don't come back.*"

All this time I'd been watching Jerry's hands as he spoke. They shook a little, but he mimed everything he was talking about—his hands on the wheel of his truck, the trees alongside the highway, his truck grinding to a halt. And when he mentioned his daughter, his hand moved so gently, as if he was stroking her hair.

"So you took a walk," I said.

"Yep. I started walking and I said the prayer my old man taught me. He was a bush pilot. Toughest bastard ever was. Went down twice in the middle of nowhere and walked out both times. The third time's what did it for him. Kaboom. No walking away from that one. When I was a kid he taught me this prayer: *I arise today through God's strength to pilot me....*"

There was more to the prayer. I didn't catch it all. Jerry's voice got thicker and harder to understand as his story went on.

"Walked a mile or two I guess," he said. "Christ was it cold. Stumbling over logs and s—t in the dark. And the trees. Jesus. Then I just stopped. Thought about my little girl. How was this gonna help her, right? So I vowed right then and there that I'd never touch another f—king drop. *You spineless piece of s—t,* I said, *you turn around and go*

142

look after that kid and never drink again and if you ever do then you come back out here and finish this for good."

I looked at the state he was in and thought that he hadn't made good on either of his pledges, but I was wrong.

"So I quit," he said. "Never drank again. Nope. Got clean and got a better-paying job at the sands. Instead of driving the highway I operated one of the big haulers. Bought my wife and kid a new house. Trip to Disneyworld. Then. Yeah. There's the stuff worse than booze. The heavy stuff. Those guys. Man. Some days it seemed we were snorting more happy powder than we were digging up tar."

Jerry spit on the sidewalk and muttered under his breath. He seemed to have forgotten I was there.

"I don't touch nothing now," he said, as if to himself. "Got it all burned out good now and I don't touch nothing."

He got up and shuffled off, mumbling to himself, his hands still miming some memory that haunted him.

I finished my lunch and then headed south through the city. It was hot and muggy and the noise and the exhaust from the cars had me strung out before long, but I kept going. I had no idea what I was looking for, but I told myself, "You'll know it when you see it." Whatever that meant.

To shorten this long story, around midnight I found myself at the border crossing into Point Roberts. As you may know, this is a tiny little neck of land that the U.S. laid claim to because it happens to fall below the forty-ninth parallel on a map. Which obliges its inhabitants to either own a boat or cross into another country in order to get to the rest of Washington State.

I went up to the guard leaning on the porch rail of his little house. I hadn't talked to anyone for hours, since my conversation with Jerry on the library steps.

"Where are you headed this evening, sir?" the guard asked.

I didn't answer him right away. I couldn't. At that moment it struck me, the absurdity of these make-believe divisions on a ball of rock that has existed for billions of years in a state of ceaseless change, where nothing has ever stayed neatly in one place, not deserts, not oceans, not forest, not continents. *This is mine, that is yours. Keep out.* Nations acting towards each other like we act towards strangers on the street, putting on this charade of separateness. Unless they've got something we want. Then we move in and take it over and pretend that it always belonged to us. All the energy we put into insisting things are real and permanent that only come and go.

"Sir?" he said. Now there was an edge to his friendliness. "I asked you where you're headed tonight."

"I'm going home," I said.

And I turned around and did just that. Well, first I slept for a couple of hours on the beach at Tsawwassen, where the Vancouver Island ferry comes in. It was pretty windy and chilly there. I stood it for as long as I could, then I got up and kept walking. I wasn't hiking at the same energetic pace on the return journey—the leg was starting to act up—so I didn't get home until after lunchtime the following day. I walked for a long time along a major road with the cars roaring past me, the people in them hurrying to whatever was important in their lives. That steady, insistent noise seemed to be where all the action was, the life. But then I looked up at the mountains and I thought about the vast movements of the earth over the millennia, the unrecorded million-year upheavals that had created those mountains, and the self-important roar and rush of the cars faded away to the buzz of insects, flashing for a moment in the sun and then gone. We're here for such a brief time.

I got to the front door and found it ajar. I froze, then I stepped inside, expecting to find an intruder. And I did. A big scruffy grey dog bounded past me out of the kitchen and hightailed it outside. Turns out I hadn't shut the door properly when I left in a hurry the day before, and he'd taken advantage of the opportunity. There was an unholy mess on the kitchen floor—the dog had gotten into the garbage I hadn't taken out before leaving. He'd eaten his fill and then expressed his appreciation for the meal by crapping voluminously in a corner.

For some reason this seemed like the punchline of an obscure joke, the kind you find funny *because* it doesn't add up. So I sat down and laughed. I knew I'd never get to those poles, I was never meant to get there, and that was all right.

I have Michael's drawing above my desk. Please thank him for me.

Nancy tells me she's going home for good at the end of the school term. Too much fresh air here, is how she put it. These are sad tidings. I've come to like having my nice, comfortable solitude disrupted.

Best wishes,
James

New York, USA
April 12, 1979

Dear James,

So glad to hear you're feeling better now. I've been thinking a lot about what you shared with me about your experience in Nepal, and here, for what they're worth, are my thoughts.

As a journalist I've heard stories of experiences similar to the one you had on the stretcher. Remember when you told me about seeing the grey whales – your colleague said it was like looking into the eye of God. And now, you could say, you've seen things from the other side of that encounter. I suppose it makes sense that if you were God, even for an instant, it would be a bit of a let-down to become merely human again. But that's probably a good thing. Being merely human, I mean. I've never had an experience like yours, but I don't think we fallible mortals are meant to know everything. We need to be surprised. By the world, by others, by ourselves. Sometimes I think that if there is a God, he or she or it isn't hiding somewhere on the other side of things. What if God is a fall off a cliff into a gorge? Or a little bit of living green inside a cracked-open rock? What if God is the surprise itself?

Anyhow, the amazing facts that you and I like to collect and share would mean nothing if we weren't open to the risk of finding out that the world isn't what we thought it was, or would like it to be. It's part of keeping alive one's sense of wonder, I suppose. I think you're going to be fine because you obviously haven't lost that.

I've heard Jerry's prayer before. One of my aunts used to recite it whenever she started off on a trip. It's called "The Deer's Cry" and it was supposed to have been written by Saint Patrick of Ireland. The legend says that Patrick was traveling to the king's court and he learned that a gang of pagan druids was lying in wait to ambush him and his fellow monks (I've made it sound a bit like a Monty Python skit, haven't I?). The visit to the king was important to Patrick, and he'd never been one to back down from danger. If he had been he never would have come to Ireland in the first place. So anyhow he had his monks all recite this prayer as they walked along the road. And the result was, the would-be saint killers waiting in ambush saw only a herd of deer passing by.

The part that Jerry recited goes like this:

I arise today, through God's strength to pilot me.
God's eye to look before me,
His wisdom to guide me,
His shield to protect me,
from temptation,
from all who shall wish me ill,
afar and near, alone and among the multitudes.
God stand with me,
against every cruel, merciless power
that may oppose my body and my soul...

You probably consider this just superstitious nonsense. Still, Patrick's miraculous prayer has been set to music and it's one of the most beautiful hymns I know. I heard it sung here once in St Patrick's Cathedral, at a relative's wedding.

I have to admit I'll be glad to have Nancy back. With her usual go-getter-ness, she's got a couple of teaching possibilities lined up here already.

The other day we celebrated my 28th birthday at Tavern on the Green in Central Park. I wasn't told where we were going until we got there. And there was an added surprise, not planned by Philip and Michael: I spotted John Lennon in the restaurant, with Yoko and their little boy. A strange moment—our little family of three and theirs, across the room from one another. Our two boys eyeing each other curiously. If the other people in the restaurant realized who they were, and I'm sure everyone did, no one was making a fuss. Philip didn't notice them, and I didn't mention it to him until after we had left. I wanted us all to just leave them alone (insert bad joke here about giving peace a chance). It looked like they were getting some time as an ordinary family, for a few blessed moments. As I sat there trying not to glance over too often, I felt I had a little insight into what it would be like to be famous—the burden that it must be when people idealize you, project their desires onto you, make you into a kind of surrogate for a missing deity, perhaps. And yet you're just the same as everyone around you. You're human. You're as vulnerable and flawed as everyone else. How lonely a life that must be at times.

In your last letter you said you were concerned that Michael would be disappointed to meet his hero in the flesh. I doubt that would be the case, but there's only one way to find out for sure, isn't there?

best wishes,
Martha

Vancouver, Canada
May 10, 1979

Dear Martha,

Your last letter reminded me of some important things I had forgotten lately, as well as pointing out things I had never considered. You're right about surprises and why we need them. And speaking of surprises, I suppose you've heard about the other night, when I talked to Michael on the phone. From what I gather, he was sleeping over at Aunt Nancy's place, and she thought it would be great for the two of us to have a little chat. Which it was. We talked about binturongs and trains and other interesting things. The conclusion we arrived at is that I should come for a visit soon. So I will.

I've got most of July free, for a change, but let me know if there is a time that would be best. I promise not to get in your way. When I get to New York you can point me in the direction of the nearest green space and I'll go looking for lichens and won't bother anyone.

Your friend,
James

New York, USA
May 19 1979

Dear James,

Yes, I was informed by Michael about Aunt Nancy's crafty little ploy. I can't say I'm unhappy about it, though. It would be so good to have you visit us, and no, you won't be in anyone's way. If you come in mid-July, Philip has his vacation days, and that way we would have plenty of time for a tour in and around the city. One place in particular that I know you would appreciate is Inwood Hill Park, up in the northwest corner of the island. I've been told this nature preserve holds the last stands of natural forest in the New York area. With a little deliberate heedlessness, one can get lost in there. I think you'd like it.

Looking forward to seeing you again,
Martha

Vancouver, Canada
June 19, 1979

Dear Martha,

Just a quick note to tell you I've made my travel plans. In case you try to reach me in the next few days, I should tell you I'm leaving tomorrow on a field research trip to the Queen Charlottes. When I get back in early July I'll be putting my notes in order for a couple of days, and then I'll be boarding a plane to New York, on the 10th.

You were right about waiting a year. The tree now stands just under an impressive ten feet, and is filling out beautifully. There must have been an outdoor wedding on the lawn recently, because there is confetti in the grass and bits of coloured streamers hanging from the branches. I wouldn't be surprised if a lot of people have their pictures taken under the tree—it stands slightly away from the others around it, so that it seems to be more of an individual.

See you soon,
your friend,
James

New York, USA
July 5 1979

Dear James,

I have terrible news. My beloved godson Michael was killed on June 29th in a car accident. Martha was on her way to her mother's house on Long Island when it happened. She and Philip had a fight earlier in the evening and she was leaving to get some time on her own. It was a rainy night and Martha was passed by a tractor-trailer that slid out of control on the wet road and slammed into her vehicle. She was injured, a broken arm and a concussion, and the driver of the truck was unhurt, but Michael was killed instantly.

I tried to contact you by phone but when I couldn't reach you I decided to write instead so you would get the news as soon as you got home. The funeral was yesterday, near Martha's mother's house on Long Island. Martha stayed with me for a couple of days but now she is back in the hospital. Her injuries were not severe, thank God, but she is not eating or sleeping and sometimes she doesn't recognize anyone. It's as if her mind and body are shutting down.

She blames herself for being distracted and not paying attention to the road conditions, although it is in no way her fault. She won't talk to Philip. All I can do is be with her and pray for the strength to see her through this.

We are all devastated and in great pain.

Nancy

2

He stood on the porch of his house in the grey morning light, holding the letter in his hand. His eyes were on the page but he wasn't taking in the words. He'd already read them again and again since finding the letter in his mailbox an hour ago.

Every single day, for months now, she had been the first thought on his mind when he woke. Every day he stopped what he was doing and wondered how she was, if she was all right.

How could she be all right?

He hadn't written to her. The one time he finally goaded himself into calling her number, weeks ago, no one had answered the phone.

Now this letter had arrived, the first from Nancy in many months.

New York, USA
March 14 1980

Dear James,

How are you? It has been so long since we've spoken to each other. I'm sorry for that. Things have been difficult here, to say the least. I'm sure I don't have to tell you what Martha has been going through. She stayed with me for several weeks after she got out of the hospital and then she moved back into the apartment with Philip, but as I feared this hasn't worked out. They've been separated for some time now and I doubt that they will ever get together again.

I don't know how much Martha confided to you about her married life but it was never a perfect dream of marital bliss. Far from it, I'm sorry to say. She probably won't be happy with me for telling you this but a few years ago Philip confessed he'd been cheating on her with a woman he'd met at work. Martha was heartbroken and she left Philip for a while, but he begged her for forgiveness and promised he would never stray again and finally she came back. I honestly think she stayed more for Michael's sake than for her marriage.

Even before Philip's infidelity came to light he and Martha fought quite a bit, usually because Philip was never around. In my opinion he was always married more to his work than to Martha, and for her part that stubborn Scottish temperament she inherited would rise up and there'd be no talking to her. Sometimes they'd go for days without speaking a word to one another. Philip can be a very controlling person as well, and expected things at home to be just so, and when they weren't he could really fly off the handle. I also think, from some of the things Martha has said, that in some way Philip was even jealous of what you and she shared. I think that was probably why she never came to see Michael's tree.

Still, I always believed that the two of them were up to pretty much every challenge of married life, until Michael died. Philip had great hopes and dreams for his son. Talking to him I've realized that even though he claims he has come to terms with what happened he still needs to find someone to blame for his pain and loss. He's lashed out at the world in my presence a couple of times, going over the events of that night, about how there should have been more weather warnings, better lights on the freeways, things like that, and once he said to me "if I'd been driving it wouldn't have happened." Which means that in some corner of his heart he believes that Martha is responsible for Michael's death. And I'm afraid she believes it too. She said to me once that she understood if Philip hated her now. How can two people stay together when there's that kind of unhealable wound between them?

The truth is, James, when it comes to Martha I am close to despair. I've tried to interest her again in the things she used to love but she won't even go look at her garden. She is working again, or trying to, but that is all she ever does now: sit at her desk and write articles on subjects she doesn't really care about. "As long as it pays the bills," is her new motto, if you can believe it. She's taken up smoking again, too, I've discovered, though she tries to hide it from me. Sometimes I just want to shake her! I visit her when I can although I'm busy with a challenging new teaching job. I try to bring Martha out, even just a little, with gossip and chatter and the usual no-brainer stuff I'm good at. Every so often I can get a smile out of her but it's the most heartbreaking sight I've ever seen. Sometimes when she's been drinking she gets furious with me and she won't return my calls for days. Not too long ago we were talking about this frightening new disease they've discovered, this AIDS (what a ridiculous acronym for something that kills people. God!), and Martha said that maybe it was better for Michael to have died than to have to grow up in a world like this, a world full of misery and violence and so many horrible unsolvable problems. Then she looked up at me and she said, "I should've died, too."

I've never heard her say anything like that, ever. I am seriously worried, James. I thought by now I'd see a little of the old Martha but little by little she's disappearing instead of coming back and I don't know what to do.

Nancy

A noise in the street made him look up.

His neighbor's teenaged son was pulling into their driveway in his beat-up Mustang. Heavy metal music blaring from the stereo. First thing in the morning? He must be just getting home after a night's partying or God knows what. The boy's mother was in the flowerbed planting tulip bulbs. She stood up when she heard him coming and walked over to the car. What was her name again? Alena? Annika? Her husband was a railway engineer. Gus ... Szabados, that was it. The boy got out of the car and had a brief conversation with the woman that James couldn't hear. He was staring at the ground and rubbing his arm while his mother did most of the talking. Then suddenly he brushed past her with a loud curse, a shocking word directed at her, and went inside, slamming the door behind him.

How old was he now? Not long ago he'd been a little boy tearing around the neighborhood riding a pretend horse, yipping and hollering. James couldn't summon up his name either. He'd been their neighbour for years and he knew hardly anything about these people.

The woman turned and saw him on his porch. She waved to him and started to walk over.

Not now, he thought, folding up the letter and pasting a smile on his face.

"Teenagers," she said with a shake of her head when she got closer. *Anezka.* She'd do this from time to time, suddenly come over when she saw him outside and launch into a mostly one-sided conversation in her terse, no-nonsense manner. At least she'd never pried into his personal life.

"Late night I guess," he said for the sake of saying something.

"Always a late night with him," she said with the trace of an Eastern European accent. "Gus and me were out at the cabin last weekend. We think he had a party while we were gone. I found a dent in the kitchen wall. He says to me *I don't know how that got there.* Ha."

Her manner was brusque but he could see the hurt in her eyes and in the set of her jaw. She was braving it out, he saw, playing the tough parent, but this was her child. The little boy who used to run around playing pretend.

"I'm sorry to hear that," he said.

"Were you here last weekend? Did you see anything?"

James hesitated. He had been at home. Where else would he be? Up late because he couldn't sleep, half-heartedly working on the revisions to a paper and telling himself he should be calling Nancy. But he hadn't. Now that he thought about it there'd been a racket outside for a while but he hadn't paid any attention. Hadn't even got up to look out the window. As if whatever happened *here* didn't matter at all.

"Well, I did hear some noise I guess," he said. "But I didn't see anything going on. Sorry."

"Okay," she said, looking away. It was clear she'd picked up on his desire to be left alone. "Okay. Thank you. Have a good day."

"Let me know the next time you and Gus go away," he called after her as she walked back across the lawn. He felt the need to make some gesture. "I'll keep an eye out."

He went inside his house and made a cup of coffee. While he sipped it mechanically, not tasting it, he went through the rest of his mail and then tucked it all away amid the heaps of books and journals and papers covering his kitchen table. The letter from Nancy he kept with him.

As he sat there he felt his plans for the morning recede. He let them go. He'd been working day and night for weeks now, struggling to finish a crucial paper. Years of work poured into this thing and he could barely summon the energy to care. Tasks that had once absorbed him—gathering and sorting his data, setting out his ideas in clear and logical sentences—now seemed to take enormous effort and no longer brought any glow of accomplishment.

He still felt the anguish of the day Nancy's letter came. The news he couldn't, *wouldn't* believe. That evening he went out to visit Michael's tree. It was all he could think to do. Rain had been falling heavily most of the day and the campus was all but deserted. He touched the pine's soft needles and reddish bark, as if the tree could somehow help him reach out to her, to where she was now, a place of suffering beyond any of his own life's losses and heartaches.

Over the next few days he debated with himself whether or not to cancel his plan to come to New York. The purpose of his visit had been to meet Michael, and he feared his showing up so soon after the funeral would only be one more painful reminder of what she had loss. In the end he talked to Nancy, who urged him to come, and so he did.

The day he came to see her, not long after the funeral. Her last day in the hospital. He stood at the door, hesitating. It was the first time he had seen her in five years, and it struck him that he had only known a part of her, the part that she put into her letters. He had come here expecting to meet that person, but the woman sitting on the edge of the bed, her back turned to him, could have been a stranger. She was so still and silent, gazing out the window, like a child lost in a daydream. The sun was shining in through the window, it was an absurdly gorgeous summer day outside, but she looked as if the light was going right through her, as if she wasn't there.

Her bags were packed and she was dressed to leave. Everything in the room neat and tidy, a brush and a small make-up bag on the bedside table, and he had a sudden realization that Nancy had done all of this. Martha had needed someone's help simply to get dressed, to brush her hair, to straighten up the room for visitors. Even these ordinary daily tasks were beyond her.

He stepped into the room, gripping the bouquet of daffodils wrapped in thin paper, afraid to disturb her and not knowing whether he should make some noise to alert her to his presence. If she had heard his earlier knock and knew someone was there, she gave no sign.

He moved closer and spoke her name. She turned and looked at him without seeming to know who he was. The first time he'd seen her face since Iceland. She was not the same person he remembered. So thin. Frail. For a moment he thought he saw a light kindle in her eyes, but it was so far off and went out so quickly. He couldn't speak. He saw that his friend, the woman whose letters had been so alive with curiosity and wonder, was alone in a place no one could reach. No one could join her there.

Before he knew what he was doing he had taken her in his arms. She was so thin, there was almost nothing to her. The fear shot through him that she was in actual physical danger of dying. He held her tightly, as if that way he could give her some of his own life. Her hands came up and gripped his arms, and for a moment all that he had felt and wished for since he first met her came welling up in him. She was here, in his arms, at last. He whispered her name, and after a moment he felt her stiffen and pull away. She sat down again, avoiding his eyes, while her hands smoothed her blue summer dress over and over.

They talked for a while longer, about what he later couldn't remember. Awkward, forced small talk. She may have asked him how his plane trip had been. She spoke very little, and he could see that she was struggling to care even a little that he was here. It was clear to him he was only making things more difficult for her. He had no right to intrude on her grief. Did he really think he mattered to her at all after *this?*

He flew home the next day and since then he had not written, had not called. He felt now that he had come to New York only out of selfishness, as an opportunity to see her once again. Their meeting in the hospital had shown him what anyone else would have accepted long before: that he would never be anything to this woman but a distant acquaintance, one who could share her interests but who had no other place in her life. Her real life, which was filled now with more pain than he had ever known or could truly understand.

He sat now at his kitchen table, surrounded by the stacks of work he'd tried to lose himself in. There was no hope for this stuff. Not now.

He threw on a coat and went for a walk by the river. After a while the sky clouded over and a soft rain began to fall. He stopped in the middle of the trail, listening. What had she told him in that letter. Philip's Uncle Henry said there was a soul in all matter, not just living things. Knock on a wall, turn a page, break a glass, you can hear the soul of a thing speaking to you. *Maybe that's why the sounds of the forest seem more meaningful to you than the sounds of the city* she'd written. He'd read it over so many times he'd memorized the words. *Precisely because the sounds in the forest are less identifiable. You don't immediately assign a human meaning to them, and so the voice of the soul of things is clearer.*

He listened to the rain pattering on the leaves. Were they saying anything? No. It was just rain. It had nothing to say to him. And why should he keep coming out here waiting for something to speak to *him*?

When he got home he changed into dry clothes, sat down at the table and cleared a space in front of him. He took out a fresh sheet of paper and a pen, and wrote *Dear Martha* beneath the letterhead and the date.

She was in need, and his letters were what he could offer her. If they were a solace, or even simply a distraction, then well and good. To hope they might mean anything more to her was ridiculous. It was better for both of them, too, if he never saw her again. He could be a true friend to her only if he kept a continent between them. If he finally gave up on this fantasy he had been nurturing for far too long, that this woman was his destiny.

He picked up one of his field notebooks, found a blank page at the end, and wrote.

You've never opened yourself to anyone. Not your whole being, like she did with her child. This is the life you've earned for never taking that risk. So get on with it.

Vancouver, Canada
March 23 1980

Dear Martha,

I hope you are well.

For years I've wanted to visit the Amazon rainforest, and it looks like I will finally get the opportunity later this year. I've signed on to an expedition with a trio of pharmacologists who are going to search for new and rumoured species of plants that might have medicinal properties. We'll spend two months travelling down the river and up again in a hired boat, crossing from Peru into Brazil and back.

I'm writing this on my porch. It's early morning. The weather is astonishingly cold for this time of year in subtropical Canada. A cement truck is trundling up the hill bright and early—a foundation is being laid for some new monster house that's going up on my block. One of the last of the weathered old survivors on this street (house and occupant both) is gone. If I hang on to my place long enough, by the looks of it, I'll be able to sell it for enough money to … to live where? I like things fine right here. Although I'm told there's a strip mall going up at the bottom of the hill, and that means new roads, and more cars.

Last night the aurora borealis was the brightest I have ever seen it. Lying on my back in a field not far from my house I felt as if my vantage point were at the centre of the whole spectacle, as if this performance were being put on just for me. The lights appeared at first from the north. They were slender, and slightly radiating as if they were being brushed softly into the night sky by a gentle hand. I was reminded of the moonbow I saw on the sea years ago. Then came soft pulses of spectral blue-green light, one after another, rising and soaring slowly upwards. They were arched in shape, but wavering slightly and with the arch seemingly broken at the top. They seemed to float, not following the curve of the atmosphere as falling stars seem to, but free, moving in their own element. Eventually, in all directions from north to south, from east to west, the lights were equally bright, and as I watched, every so often, with a tremulous motion these immense iridescent sheets would roll slowly, like sea waves, from horizon to horizon.

As an experiment I took out a book (it happened to be the compact edition of Shakespeare's complete works that Nancy had given me before she left), and discovered I was able to read by the light of the aurora.

Please give Nancy my best wishes.

Your friend,
James

Vancouver, Canada
July 14 1980

Dear Martha,

I am writing to give you news from the Queen Charlotte Islands. The Haida and their supporters have won a small but significant victory in their struggle against the logging industry. A protected area has been created, encompassing the northwest corner of Graham Island, which the people themselves will manage.

Clarence and I were invited to the ribbon-cutting ceremony, which turned out to be a ribbon-tying ceremony, actually. A symbolic length of cedar bark twine was knotted together at the entrance to the park, as a symbol that this place was now a protected sanctuary.

As I was walking back to my hotel from the ceremony, a man who I assume works for the logging industry came up to me and spit right in my face, then called me some ugly names. I didn't feel any anger, oddly enough. That teenager who used to jump in at the drop of a hat with both fists flying is long, long gone. I took out my handkerchief, wiped my face, and walked away, feeling sad more than anything else.

I typed this letter on a personal computer at the university. It's no secret that we're at the beginning of a new era with these devices. Technophiles predict that in a few years just about everybody will have a computer in their home, and that offices will no longer use paper. A great thing for the forests, if it really comes true, which I doubt. I don't think we can do without our piles of paper. We stack them up on our desks like fortifications. They also say that eventually, maybe in the next ten years, people will communicate over phone lines with one another via computer, in a great invisible electronic web of information exchange. No stamps, no paper. Just words and pictures on screens, coming from everywhere and going everywhere without a centre anywhere. Like the universe, I suppose. Whether this super-network is something to be alarmed or excited about is difficult to say. I like the idea of being able to share discoveries with other scientists across borders in no time at all but I can also imagine the potential for a "web" like this to spread misinformation and just plain garbage. When there's too much information, too much noise, how do you take anything meaningful in? How do you even see it?

At any rate I hope you don't mind if I go on writing letters, no matter what form they take in future.

Your friend,
James

Vancouver, Canada
October 5 1980

Dear Martha,

I hope you are well.

I've been busy making sure all is in order for the Amazon trip. It has meant an astonishing amount of red tape—Jean-Pierre and the other pharmacologists want to be absolutely sure that we have all of the permits and other documents we need to hack our way through the bureaucratic jungle. These days it seems an expedition has to be more concerned about paper than food and gear.

Here's an odd thing. An oceanographer I know told me recently about unusual sound waves that have been detected in the Pacific Ocean. They're called "t-waves" and they're among the purest sounds ever heard in nature, in the sense that they are limited to a very narrow frequency of 3 to 12 cycles per second. These deep bass rumblings can last a few seconds or minutes at a time, and no one is really sure what's causing them. One dubious theory has it that the sounds come from the lost city of Atlantis, and that the Atlanteans (evolved to become water-breathers) are soon to rise and share their wondrous technology with us surface dwellers. My oceanographer acquaintance believes otherwise: he says the sounds are likely from a the periodic venting of an undersea volcano.

Your friend,
James

Iquitos, Peru
January 2 1981

Dear Martha,

We're nearly at the end of our two month cruise along the Amazon. I'm flying home in a few days.

Our journey started out and has ended in Iquitos, a town in northern Peru, east of the Andes, that was once a bustling port for the rubber trade. We hired a weathered-looking riverboat, the *Utopía*, captained by a bushy-bearded, piratical-looking man by the unlikely name of MacTavish. He had a crew of two taciturn young Indians, brothers, neither of whom spoke any language we could speak, and my companions were collectively fluent in many. Just when we were about to leave Iquitos the pharmacologists hired a guide, a Mestizo named Orfeo, a slight, sinewy man of about forty or so, who swore to us with deep seriousness that he knew the river as if it were his mother. Foster, one of the pharmacologists, started calling him "Mama's boy" behind his back, but the joke soon turned into a term of respect when it became obvious he hadn't been idly boasting. Even MacTavish started depending on Orfeo for details of the current and the depth and so on.

The senior partner of the pharmacology trio, Jean-Pierre Roussel, brought his wife with him. Her name's

Marina Kostopoulos and she's a professional photographer. She told me there was no way she was going to let her husband take a once-in-a-lifetime trip like this without her. I confess I had some chauvinistic doubts at first about the wisdom of having her along, but they were quickly dispelled. She dealt with the heat and the bugs and the intestinal troubles etc with far less grousing than we big brave menfolk did.

The riverboat travelled at night as well as during the day. At night we strung our hammocks on the deck as the boat chugged along in the darkness, and before we fell asleep we picked out the constellations of the southern hemisphere. Most of the time, where the river was quite wide, we weren't bothered by insects to a great degree, although one night we passed through a storm of alarmingly large black beetles, buzzing and clattering their wings and landing on every available surface, including our skin and hair, that sent all of us *turistas* scrambling below decks.

Since this was not a luxury cruise the meals never varied: chicken, rice, beans, tomatoes, all stewed together with lots of spices. I had to eat it if I didn't want to go hungry, but I would scoop the chicken out of my bowl and put it back into the communal pot. They all thought I was crazy for doing that. The fare was sometimes supplemented with fresh-caught fish, which I admit I tried, and it was quite good. Breakfast, without fail, was a thick, salty porridge and whatever fruit we happened to gather the day before.

At times the boat stopped so that we could explore the surrounding terrain. Although only Jean-Pierre is French, I soon named the pharmacologists the Three Musketeers—to myself, that is—for their manly posturing (they had Marina take lots of pictures of them standing at the prow of the boat with hands on hips etc) and their swashbuckling way of collecting specimens: hauling themselves up trees with rope and tackle, slashing through underbrush, wandering off by themselves into the pathless bush. Sometimes they needed an extra hand, and since I was usually nearby I found myself pressed into service more than once. Whether that made me d'Artagnan I don't know.

It is beyond belief what riches and surprises a single tree in this forest can hold. There are different living communities at every level, from the roots to the high canopy. One tree alone can be home to more species of ants than there are in all of Canada. The Amazon region is good for all kinds of superlatives, of course. The river is 300 feet deep in places; that's deep enough to submerge the Statue of Liberty. The largest moth in the world is found here, the Owlet moth, with a wingspan up to twelve inches. As is the largest leaf, that of the bamboo palm, which can grow up to 65 feet long. The Amazon is the home of the smallest monkey, the pygmy marmoset, which some people keep in their hair to get rid of lice and other insect pests, and some of the world's tiniest frogs, which can be smaller than the word "frog" I've just written on this page.

Have you ever seen pictures of the red-faced monkey, the uakari? They're also known as the "English monkey," and I understand the nickname goes back to colonial times, when drunken, cursing, miserable Englishmen were a fairly common sight in these parts.

There are about eight thousand species of birds in the world, and more than half of them are found in the Amazon basin. We zoom all over the world in planes these days, but birds are the real travellers. I like to imagine the way they must see what we think of as a human world: for days and days they fly over forests, deserts, mountain ranges, seas, and then, here and there comes a village, a town, a city. To them, these are patches of non-life, to be avoided. The opposite of how we see the world most of the time, but for the same reason: they're looking for what's useful to them.

Another Amazonian record-breaker: nearly forty percent of the world's species of freshwater fish are native to the Amazon River basin. There are more different kinds of fish in the river than there are in the entire Atlantic Ocean. And there are many many species of animal and plant that remain to be discovered, so that in years to come a lot of these "biggest, longest, smallest" records will likely be superseded by new discoveries. That is, if there is still a rainforest for them to be discovered in. It's being cut down at a frightening rate for farming and ranching.

Along the way, through the mediation of Orfeo, we encountered various Indios who knew a great deal about which plants were useful for medicines. We learned, for example, that the skin of the boa constrictor is useful as a treatment for wounds. And there is a certain climbing vine whose sap has a paralyzing effect. The Indios dip their arrowheads in the sap to shoot monkeys out of trees. The arrows aren't powerful enough to guarantee a kill, but in a few minutes the sap does its work and the monkeys fall out of the branches, unable to move. For me the best proof of what the jungle can do came as we left a town called Tonantins: either from food or drink or who knows what I contracted something that turned fairly nasty. I was feverish and nauseated and couldn't hold down much more than thin broth. After a couple of days of this, with nothing in the pharmacologists' own supply helping much, Orfeo had us stop at a small town, a seedy-looking place that seemed to be the rubbish dump for the entire region. Old cars, appliances, mounds of burning trash, tin cans. The aroma of all this garbage didn't help my stomach.

Orfeo came back with a smelly, greenish-black concoction that he called "tea" and urged me to drink. Abandoning myself to fate I choked the pulpy stuff down and that night I felt worse than ever, to the point where I wasn't sure I was going to make it out of here alive. But the next morning the symptoms had lessened a great deal, and by evening I was dining with the others again.

The three musketeers had Orfeo list the ingredients of this marvelous beverage, and I have the recipe now, though it's not something you could easily put together anywhere but here.

We found that the most active time for birds and animals in the jungle was between sunrise and about ten in the morning. After that, the stultifying heat drives most of the wildlife to shelter and rest. So I got in the habit of rising at 4:30 every morning and helping the captain (who doubled as cook) with breakfast. I've been keeping a list of the birdlife we encounter: white and black and red herons, vultures, swifts, kingfishers, ibises, ospreys, terns, pigeons, at least seven different species of woodpecker, beautiful red and green macaws. The trip's pretty much over but the list keeps growing. My favourite: the toucan. A bird that's mostly beak with the rest of the body as an appendage. Its glassy red-rimmed eyes and ragged crest make it look like it just got jolted awake after a night of carousing.

I had a run-in one day with these birds. I was on my hands and knees in a thicket, examining the litter on the forest floor for lichens, when I surprised a toucan concealed in the leaves. Why it was on the ground I don't know, maybe it was injured, but anyhow it set up a loud scream. In an instant, even though there hadn't been a sign of them before, the thicket was alive with toucans. They flapped down from the vines and branches overhead, hopping from bough to bough, some of them swinging in the loops and cables of the lianas, all of them squawking at me, fluttering their wings and raising their "hackles" furiously. I beat a hasty retreat and a few moments later, from a safe vantage point, I watched them climb back up into the trees, where they disappeared again from view.

As we travelled, sometimes we would pass a village and the older children would paddle out in dug-out canoes and then stand up in them, trying to surf in the wake of the boat. We cheered them on, and threw chocolate bars and coins to whoever got close enough.

The pink dolphin of the Amazon is the last thriving river dolphin in the world. The people along the river have all kinds of superstitions about them, including the idea that they can leave the water at night, take human form, and have sex with sleeping men. No one in our little troupe reported any such nocturnal visitations. Marina speculated this was a version of the myth of the succubus, which I'd never heard of before. She also called it typical patriarchal baloney: something elusive and beautiful and mysterious must be female, and therefore dangerous. So then it's okay to kill it.

Finally we arrived in Manaus, a big port city bustling with vessels of all shapes and sizes, including gigantic cargo ships that come in from the Atlantic. There is a huge fish market in this town, where anything that can be found in the river can be bought for dinner. The ornate opera house that was built here in the nineteenth century is closed and in a poor state, although there are plans to renovate it and bring in touring companies again.

On the return trip, listening to the musketeers talk with Orfeo in Spanish, I caught odd bits of conversation about a *brujo*, which my Spanish dictionary informed me means "sorcerer." What in the world were they up to? I kept eavesdropping and slowly pieced together what they'd really been most keen about on this trip. They're pharmacologists. I should have known. Anyhow, near the town of Tabatinga they got what they were after. Orfeo led us by raft up a tributary to a Tikuna village and introduced us to an old man in a straw cowboy hat and dusty blue track suit, Don Rafael. Apparently he's a shaman who heals people with various plant medicines. After some discussion and bartering—the Musketeers gave the village some of our food and medical supplies—Don Rafael agreed to let us participate in a ceremony involving the hallucinogenic vine known as *ayahuasca*, or *yagé*, which the Tikuna boil up with various other herbal ingredients into a healing drink. William Burroughs wrote about the stuff in the Fifties, it appears. I was never interested in his stuff though all my college friends read him. The Three Musketeers knew his writings on the subject and were eager to try the drug for themselves.

Marina declined. She saw this as some kind of male bonding/initiation thing that she wanted no part of. My sense was that Jean-Pierre didn't want her joining in anyhow. I admit I was intrigued but still shaky from my illness. I was also thinking of my experience in the hospital in Nepal. So I decided I'd better abstain. This was fine with the Musketeers, who saw an opportunity to have someone remain lucid and watch the proceedings with scientific objectivity. The shaman seemed unsure about this arrangement, but in the end he agreed that I could stay as an observer. My job would be to man the tape recorder and keep a notebook handy. We waited in the village "square" until evening, and just about everyone in Don Rafael's extended family took a break from what they were doing to come have a gander at these bizarre foreigners.

Finally the old man led us into the *maloca* or ceremony house, a round structure of wood and a kind of South American bamboo called guadua. We were welcomed by his wife, a thin, astonishingly wrinkled old woman with an irrepressible smile. Marina came in, too, to take some "before" photos, as she put it. When we entered, the old woman ushered us each to a woven mat on the floor and gave each of us a small cushion, for our heads when we lay down later, as Orfeo translated for us. I noticed there was a plastic pail beside each mat and I wasn't sure what they were for, but it became clear later.

The old woman was talkative and fussed around us, clearly anxious to please her guests. There seemed to be no rush for things to get started, then all of a sudden though she was hurrying Marina out the door, having apparently picked up on some signal we didn't notice that her husband was ready to begin the ceremony. I asked Orfeo later if women were allowed to participate if they wanted to—he said they were.

The light was dim in the *maloca* now, only a few candles here and there, their light muted by bowls of smoked glass. Don Rafael, who was now bare-chested and dressed only in a kind of skirt, began the evening with a few prayers (I'm going by Orfeo's interpretation here). Then he brought out a big plastic Coke bottle filled with a thick-looking, brownish liquid. Foster laughed and said quietly "well it must be the real thing then," which I didn't understand. But I thought it was so wonderfully unpretentious to keep the sacred potion in a pop bottle—or as you Americans say, a soda bottle. I started to warm up to this mysterious "sorcerer."

Don Rafael went around the room and asked each participant what their intention was. Did they have a question they wanted to ask of the ayahuasca? (from what I could understand of his Spanish he spoke of the drug as if it was a "she"). Were they seeking something or looking for healing, he wanted to know. Orfeo and the Musketeers gave their answers, some of which surprised me. After that the shaman poured a small amount of the concoction into a wooden cup for each of them, and they drank. Then he took a drink himself and told everyone to sit or lie down, as they pleased, while he started to chant.

Not much happened for a while, then the participants, one after another, threw up in their plastic pail. It seems this stuff is hard on the stomach. After they'd

178

gotten that out of the way the Musketeers talked quietly about what they were experiencing. Some could see lights and colours, or hear things out in the forest, tiny little sounds they'd never noticed before. After a while they were off in their own private worlds, murmuring to themselves, and I was left behind. One was hunched over, gazing at the floor, another lying down and staring up at the roof, another rocking slowly back and forth. Sometimes they cried out and pointed, or grasped at things I couldn't see. When that happened Don Rafael went to them and put his hand on their heads and chanted softly to them. Sometimes he blew on their foreheads or took their hands in his. I wanted to ask the Musketeers what they were experiencing at those moments but it was part of the agreement that I wouldn't speak unless spoken to. At one point whatever Orfeo was seeing had him almost doubled up with laughter. The next day, after much prodding, he told us that he'd watched the *brujo* turn into a jaguar and rush out of the *maloca*, but the transformation had only gone partway and the old man's back end was all-too humanly bare as he bounded off into the forest.

One of the Musketeers, Albert (or "Aramis" as I dubbed him privately), eventually noticed me, or remembered I was there. He got up and came over to me with this look of joy and awe on his face. I wasn't supposed to say anything so I just waited.

"The plants live on light," he said, bending close to me. "The plants eat light."

I nodded, thinking to myself he was talking in a poetic way about photosynthesis. Okay, fine. Nothing totally out to lunch about that.

"That's what we call it, photosynthesis," he said, as if he'd read my mind. "But we don't *see* it. We can't see it, because it *is* what we are. *She* is showing me this. She loves us all. It's all waves of her energy. The plants live on light, we live on the plants. We are light. Energy. And the energy is love. Pure love. Everything is pure love."

He straightened up and raised his head to the ceiling. To my surprise I heard him weeping softly. So I broke my vow of silence and asked him if he was okay.

He looked back down at me, with an expression of what I can only call profound sorrow.

"You shouldn't be here," he said, placing a hand on my shoulder. "Don't you see that?"

I'd already been feeling like the only sober person at a party, looking on as everyone else gets progressively more maudlin and ridiculous. And now this expression of pity or condescension or whatever it was really annoyed me. I shrugged my shoulders and said, "Well, you wanted me here." I think he understood I was irritated—he just smiled wistfully, like someone who realizes he hasn't been understood, then he withdrew back into his personal phantasmagoria and didn't talk again. When I reported this incident to him the next morning, Albert looked truly mystified and said he couldn't remember what he'd been talking to me about.

The strangest part of the evening came when Jean-Pierre began to shake and babble in French, then raised his hands as if trying to ward something off. No one else—not Don Rafael or the other pharmacologists—took any notice. The man was clearly terrified of something and on the brink of panic. I couldn't just sit there and watch this so I went over to Jean-Pierre and put a hand on his shoulder and asked him if he was all right. All of a sudden I felt, very distinctly and without a doubt, a warm hand on the back of my neck. I whirled around – no one was near me, no one was touching me. But Don Rafael was staring right at me from across the room with a look that said as clear as day, *Leave him be*. I have to say that gave me the shivers, but it also made me angry. I wasn't going to let somebody suffer through whatever this was without trying to help. So I turned back to Jean-Pierre and put my hand back on his shoulder and told him it was okay, there was nothing to be afraid of. He called his wife's name and groped around for her as if he was blind. I told him I would take him to Marina and helped him up and out the door, all the while avoiding eye contact with Don Rafael, who I admit had me good and spooked by this point.

Marina was sitting by herself on the steps of the verandah. The old woman was nowhere to be found. When we appeared Marina jumped up and took the sobbing, shivering Jean-Pierre in her arms and sat him back down while he wept and clutched her like a frightened little boy.

"What's going on in there?" she asked me with an accusing look.

I told her I didn't know, but that Jean-Pierre had called for her.

"Stupid men," she whispered. "You think you know yourselves."

She went on speaking to her husband with comforting words and I heard him beg her forgiveness – that much of his choked babbling I was able to understand. This was clearly none of my business so I went back inside the house to keep an eye on the others. Don Rafael was staring straight ahead and didn't look at me. Which was just fine.

The rest of it was a long, mostly uneventful night and I dozed off a few times. Eventually the others came back to themselves, just as the sun was coming up. Don Rafael wasn't there—he had left the house at some point when I wasn't paying attention. I thought that was a pretty clichéd magician's trick, vanishing mysteriously, but at the same time I had no rational explanation for what he'd done, or had seemed to do, the night before. His wife came in with breakfast and told us he was gone for the day and wouldn't be back.

We left some money and returned to the boat and headed back upriver to Iquitos. Nobody spoke much that day. I felt hung over and spaced out from lack of sleep. And everyone else was pretty subdued now. Conversations short and to the point. Perfunctory. Maybe we'd all realized the trip was pretty much over now. Nothing that happened from here on was likely to top what we'd seen and experienced already. Or maybe we were all just tired of each other.

Back in Iquitos we got our first news in weeks from the rest of the world, and heard about the shooting of John Lennon.

The Musketeers need my help unloading their specimens from the boat, so I have to go. It just occurred to me that it's really going to be good to get home.

I feel like I should end this letter with some quirky or amazing fact , but for once I'm at a loss. Or maybe there's simply too much here already. Yesterday evening I was looking through Shakespeare again—I brought him with me, but haven't taken the time to read until now—and I came across a line that made me think of you.

When you do dance, I wish you a wave of the sea.

I suppose this line is an amazing fact from nature, too. Human nature and its boundless creativity. I was browsing here and there in the book and I didn't pay attention to where I read this, so I'm not sure what play it's from. To be honest I'm not really sure what the line even means, but I remember you telling me that as a kid you wanted to be a dancer when you grew up. So I thought I would send this wish to you.

Your friend,
James

New York, USA
May 10 1981

Dear James,

I want to thank you for the letters you have been sending over the past months. I haven't acknowledged them as I should have, so I'm writing now to tell you that I've appreciated every one. Please forgive this long silence. It's taken me a long time to find my way back into the world.

I am glad to hear about the new protected area on Graham Island. It must have been a satisfying moment for you, and I wish I could have been there to share it.

I'm working again as a journalist, and I live on my own now. I think Nancy has told you some of the story of how that has come about, so I won't go into the details. Philip and I are in the midst of divorce proceedings right now. Not a happy business, and I've been playing hermit from all of it for the past week, at the cottage. Mom had to go into the city for some minor surgery a few days ago, and fortunately it all went fine. She's still in the hospital so I'm alone out here for the first time. Which is a surprising thought, that I've never stayed at the cottage by myself.

This evening as the tide was going out I went for a walk along the shore, something I haven't done since before Michael died. I had been thinking about your last letter, from the Amazon, and your kind and lovely wish. I thought I would look at the waves and see what they might tell me about Shakespeare's mysterious image, which

Nancy tells me comes from *A Winter's Tale*. The sun was setting and in the southeast, over the sea, stretched a long, high bank of blueblack cloud. The tide was out and there were gulls everywhere, strutting, feeding and squawking at each other in the shallows. It might have been the scent of a change in the weather, I don't know, but once in a while there would be a general alarm and hundreds of gulls would flap up into the air. They caught the slanting golden light as they circled, gleaming white against the dark cloudbank. It made me think of a wheeling galaxy of stars.

As I was walking back to the cottage I heard a rustling sound and stopped to look for the source. In the tall dry sedges next to the road I found a gull, nestled down as if trying to conceal itself. When it heard me approach it tried unsuccessfully to hop away, and then I saw that it had a fishhook sticking through the web of one foot. Some fishing line was still attached to the hook, too, and had snagged and knotted among the grass stalks. The bird was clearly exhausted—who knows how long it had been enduring this torment. I picked the gull up, held it tight under one arm, and as gently as I could I removed the hook and unwound the line that was coiled around its leg. When I was finished I set the bird down, expecting it to flee, but it simply sat there, calmly resting and seemingly not bothered by my presence. I backed away and waited a few minutes, but the bird stayed where it was. I recalled reading that some birds will attack a wounded member of their flock, and I thought that may have been why it was trying to hide. I couldn't just leave, so I wrapped the gull in my jacket and carried it into the house. I laid it on an old sweater in a corner of the kitchen and gave it some bread and a dish of water. It stayed in a state of quiet watchfulness for the rest of the day. It nibbled at the bread but wouldn't touch the water.

Later, as I was getting ready for bed, the gull started to stir and flap its wings. I watched from the front room while it padded in slow circles around the kitchen, preening itself and ruffling its feathers, then sat down again to rest, then got up again and circled. I made some coffee and sat up all night at the table while my houseguest rested and walked around and rested some more. In the morning I opened the kitchen door, and after a short deliberation, strutting anxiously back and forth in the doorway, the gull walked outside, made a short hop, flapped its wings and took off into the morning fog.

I understood its impulse to hide. I've felt the same way for so long now. Not from a sense of menace, I mean, but just the urge to withdraw, to get *under* something so that life can't strike you any more blows. It's either that, or the only other possible escape, to just walk into the dark. Which seems so close at times that you feel you're halfway there already.

I'm also writing because there's something I need to say about the day you visited me in the hospital. I think that you went away with the wrong impression and it has been weighing on my heart ever since. When you held me close and I pulled away I could see the hurt in your eyes. I think you believed I didn't want you there, that you had done something wrong and only caused me more pain. I want you to know that is the furthest thing from the truth, and

I'm sorry it's taken me so long to tell you then what I was really feeling. Since I lost Michael I have tried hard not to feel anything, and until recently I've succeeded all too well.

When I turned and saw you that day, my heart felt something other than darkness for the first time since the night I lost my little boy. I saw the concern and sadness on your face and I knew that although we have met face to face only a few times you have been the friend to whom I've confided things I've never told anyone else, not even Nancy. I always trusted that no matter what, there was someone who really understood me. The real me.

This is very hard to say. Maybe I shouldn't be saying it at all. When you took me in your arms that day I came so close to letting go, to letting myself hide from the grief by letting the body take what it wanted. Do you understand? Even if you might feel the same way, it would have been wrong. It would have been cowardice on my part. I would have been using you.

I'm sorry to burden you with this but I hope you know that your friendship is important to me. I'll close with a request: please let me know how tall the tree is this year. I think it's time for me to come and see it.

Your friend,
Martha

Vancouver, Canada
May 16 1981

Dear Martha,

Burden me all you want. And there's nothing to forgive.

You're right about the gull—if it had returned too soon to the flock its impaired movements would have marked it out for attack. I have no doubt you improved its chances of survival.

The tree is just under fifteen feet high this year, and has filled out remarkably. It would be wonderful to see you again, and to show you the tree. Let me know when you're planning to come and I will make sure that I'm here. I'm also happy to help with travel arrangements if need be.

I was at the university all day. I'm serving on a committee that's revising the first-year curriculum, and as usual we find ourselves in opposing camps with radically different visions of what impressionable young minds need to know. After the stirring clash—sorry, *dance*—of ideologies was finally over I dragged myself home, and found your letter waiting. So I would call it a *very* good day.

Looking forward to seeing you.

Your friend,
James

New York, USA
June 1 1981

Dear James,

If I'm not mistaken, I think our conversation the other day was the first time we've talked on the phone, ever. Strange to be talking instead of writing. Hearing your voice after so long was a reminder of how kind you have been.

Thank you again for your kind offer, but I've decided to stay at the hotel as I originally planned. I think you can understand why. I will be there on the fourth anniversary of my Michael's death, and I need to feel that there will be some place where I can be completely on my own if things get overwhelming.

While I was writing this letter Nancy called to let me know she's just gotten engaged. She and her fiancé, Tony, have been pretty serious for a year now (well, as serious as Nancy can be). Tony's a great guy, fun-loving and open-hearted and more than up to the adventure of Nancy. They haven't set a date yet but have confirmed that the wedding will be here in New York. Tony is originally from England, and Nancy tells me he's got a job offer in London and wants to take Nancy back there to live. And she wants to go! I'm so happy for her, but if she does leave I'm not sure what I'm going to do without her.

Thank you for your kindness and understanding.

Looking forward to our meeting,
Martha

From Martha Geddes' diary

June 28, 1981

I've met with James. It was raining and already getting dark when I arrived, so we didn't go to see the tree. We'll do that tomorrow morning. James took me for a late dinner and I met Clarence, who does have a lovely voice and is quite handsome. Nancy was right. At one point during the meal I joked that I'd come an awful long way just to look at one tree, and Clarence told me there was an old saying among his people: "The further you go for medicine the stronger it will be." Then he winked as if he was putting me on. Maybe it was just something he'd made up on the spot. But it was good to hear.

After dinner James drove us around the bay in his rusty old van to look at the lights of the city reflecting in the water. Then they dropped me off here at the hotel. It occurs to me now that James probably brought a friend along for moral support. He probably imagined he'd have to deal with a blubbering wreck of a woman right from the moment I got off the plane. And when I caught sight of the two of them in the arrivals hall, my first horrible thought was "here's the Lone Ranger and Tonto to save the day." Rather than a burst of tears I had to fight back a fit of the giggles. The blubbering wreck hasn't made her appearance yet. We'll see how things go tomorrow.

Seeing James again has stirred up feelings in me that weren't entirely unexpected. All evening I kept wishing that

Clarence hadn't come along, that James and I could have been alone together, then I felt guilty for feeling this way. Today I faced something in myself that I'd always tried to hide from. I care for him as a friend, but I can't deny that my feelings go deeper. When I look at him things within me that have been dead for a long time come back to life. I yearn to be close to him, to be held and loved by him, body and soul. How difficult life was with Philip, how unhappy we made each other. If only I'd had the courage I would have confessed my feelings to James long ago, and things might have been different. I sometimes even let myself imagine that if I'd followed my heart Michael would be alive today.

To quote Nancy's beloved bard, that way madness lies.

I can hardly bear to be alone with thoughts like this. In the state I'm in right now it would be so easy for me to turn to James for comfort and let it become something more. I could just tell myself afterwards that I didn't know what I was doing. But even if he didn't push me away, if he returned my feelings, I know it would be selfish and wrong. I tell myself I shouldn't be having these thoughts. That's not why I'm here.

Why am I here? I feel like this has been a stupid, selfish mistake. But I have to see it through.

New York, USA
July 1 1981

Dear James,

I know I said this before I left Vancouver, but I am so grateful for all that you and Clarence did to make me welcome. What I don't think I expressed very well was how important the visit was for me.

You were so kind and considerate the whole time. I'm embarrassed to say I was close to tears from that alone. The day we went to see the tree was so gloriously brilliant, with the sailboats in the bay and the snowcapped mountains across the Strait and the tree standing so tall and green at the edge of the sea. The place you chose for the tree is so beautiful. But all I could feel was the emptiness I'd been feeling for so long, only so much worse. It's terrible to say but the beauty of the spot, of the place where you live, was like being torn open again because Michael was not with me to see it and share it with me, and he never would be. I'm sorry if this sounds ungrateful. It isn't meant to be. I truly appreciate what you were trying to do for me. I just need to be honest about my feelings in this.

I was afraid before I even arrived that this visit might finally force me to face the fact that my child is truly gone, and it did. If you hadn't been there, I'm not sure what might have happened to me. And yet somehow I think this is a good thing.

Love,
Martha

New York, USA
August 19 1981

Dear James, AKA Miracle-worker! Martha is coming to life again! I'm so happy, and so thankful. When she got back from Vancouver she came to stay with me and we had a long long talk. She told me all about her visit and how painful it was, and how kind you were.

This letter, by the way, is also a wedding invitation. Tony and I are getting married on December 1st (my birthday) at "the little church around the corner." Martha knows the one I mean. And yes it's a real honest-to-goodness church with pews and everything. Nope, no vows over a bundle of sweetgrass under the moon. The nature girl is reformed and back to her old ways. Mostly. Everyone I haven't alienated yet will be in attendance. Let's see, that'd be Martha, Mom and Aunt Hannah. And you, if you dare. RSVP.

I was going to send you a formal invitation but it just didn't seem right. I had too much to say. Tony has been in London for a couple of weeks now, preparing a place for us to live. Yes, I'm leaving dear dirty NY again. This time for good (maybe). I finally feel that I can. That visit to Vancouver was a crucial time for Martha. I don't know if you understand how crucial. A few months ago I was having serious second thoughts about moving to England and leaving Martha on her own here (her circle of friends has diminished to pretty much zero over the past couple of years). There was a time not so long ago when I honestly didn't know from one day to the next what might happen, whether she would still be there when I came to visit.

Now I really believe she'll be okay. Thank you for your part in that.

So, Encyclopedia Brown, any strange or little-known facts about England to prepare me for this mad venture into the Kingdom of Kippers-on-Toast?

Love and smooches,
Nancy

Vancouver, Canada
August 26, 1981

Dear Nancy,

Your news about Martha makes me happier than I can say. And my warmest congratulations to you and Tony. Of course I'll be at your wedding, although I won't be able to stay long. I've finally got the funding for that Antarctic trip and my plane is leaving, with or without me, 72 hours after you and Tony tie the knot.

As requested, a fact which may not be of any practical use to you, but anyhow here it is: all the swans in England, or so I've been told, are the property of the Queen. The only exception occurs every July at the Swan Upping ceremony which, like so many English terms, sounds vaguely obscene. All of the mute swans on the Thames are counted and marked for ownership either by the Crown or by the Vintners' and the Dyers' associations, both of which have an ancient privilege to claim a few birds for themselves. It all seems very archaic and pointless to me, but then so does most of what people do in the name of status and ownership. He said, working himself up to a lecture. Sorry.

Anyhow, there's my valuable and practical advice: do not eat the swans. Although given the legendary badness of the food in England, they might be your only recourse.

Best of luck,
James

Vancouver, Canada
August 26, 1981

Dear Martha,

I've just received a wedding invitation from Nancy and I'm planning to attend, of course, but all she would say about the location was that it was at a "little church around the corner." She tells me you know the place she's talking about.

I'm very much looking forward to seeing you again at the wedding. Unfortunately, as I told Nancy, my visit will be all too brief. After braving the wilds of New York I'm going on a slightly less daunting journey. I just got the news that my research grant has come through and I'll be spending a month at McMurdo Station in Antarctica, with forays into the Dry Valleys, the only part of the continent not covered by ice. I will be there for two months over Christmastime, the height of summer at the South Pole.

To make up for my hasty departure I will plan to arrive in New York a couple of days early. It's going to be crazy at that time of year though, since I'll be finishing up a term of teaching as well as preparing for the trip.

Your friend,
James

New York, USA
September 5, 1981

Dear James,

I'm very much looking forward to seeing you again, too.

Nancy is referring to the Church of the Transfiguration, on East 29th Street, between Fifth and Madison Avenues. Don't worry, when you come for the wedding I'll help you find the place. The church apparently got its nickname back in the 1800's when the minister of a more fashionable church on Fifth Avenue refused to hold a funeral service for an actor, a disreputable profession in those days. The minister snootily suggested that the actor's friends try "the little church around the corner."

The church buildings surround a lovely garden, one of my favorite quiet spots in a busy part of town.

It will be so good to have you here for as long as we can, but your trip comes first, obviously, so don't take time away from your preparations that you can't spare. Someday we'll have a chance to take that tour of New York I once promised you. Besides which, it probably won't be all that green here on the day of Nancy's wedding. Let's hope it'll be warmer than Antarctica.

Antarctica! That's wonderful—you've been looking forward to this for so long. Once again I envy you. I'm always telling you that, aren't I? Of course I say that without ever having been there, but like any other remote place the South Pole holds a fascination for me. It appeals to my sense of fairness is that Antarctica is the one place on earth that hasn't been claimed and colonized and fenced-in by a single nation. From what I understand, there are stations in Antarctica manned by countries from all over the world, even some from China. One can be optimistic and look at this as a promising sign of international cooperation. Or pessimistically, too, I suppose, as the usual jockeying of world powers to get their piece of the (frozen) pie while they can.

I just had a brilliant idea. I do get them once in a while. One of these days I want to interview you, for my "science" feature. Not when you come here for Nancy's wedding, since there likely won't be time for it then. And maybe not just about Antarctica, but about your work in general as an ecologist, and all the rare experiences you've had as a result of your chosen vocation. I don't know why this has never occurred to me before. I've enjoyed your letters so much over the years, I have no doubt others would find your work fascinating, too. I know that being put in a spotlight probably would not appeal to you, so don't feel you have to agree. If you're at all interested, we can talk about it when you get here.

See you in December,
Martha

Vancouver, Canada
September 19 1981

Dear Martha,

I've only been interviewed a few times before, by rather hostile or at least skeptical journalists. I don't know how terrific an interviewee I make, honestly but I'm willing to try it again. Spending an hour or two talking with you, even if I was forced to talk about myself, is not something I would pass up. Anyhow, I'm glad to hear you are writing again.

On the subject of conversation, I've heard that African elephants can communicate with each other over long distances, miles in fact, by the use of calls in the infrasound range. These are sound waves below the threshold of human hearing.

Your friend,
James

New York, USA
October 3 1981

Dear James,

I've been looking over my so-called science articles, with the crazy notion of making a book out of them. Something struck me about the person who wrote all these words. That busy young woman who looked at the world in such a cheerfully rational manner. As if it could all be explained with just a little digging. I envy her. But I was pretty critical of her work, too. The human body she spent so much time describing as complex and fascinating wasn't actually alive. It was an anonymous collection of working parts. She had done an expert job of not paying attention to the body she lived in, or her own life, for that matter.

I don't know if there's a book in all of this stuff, but there'd have to be a piece added to it, approaching the world from another perspective than that of complexity. That's a word for machines. I don't know of a word in English for what I'm getting at. It would have to be a word for a way of seeing what it's like to be alive from the inside, from what it's like to *be*. To be a living thing, and feel it, and marvel at it. I'm probably getting in over my head with this.

Best wishes,
Martha

Vancouver, Canada
October 16 1981

Dear Martha,

From the brief time I've spent in the Arctic I've come to realize how much language is shaped by place. As living things evolve in response to the pressures of their environment, so do languages. The Inuit apparently have no word to differentiate human beings from other living things; in other words, no "it." What I'd like to think this means—and I'm making a completely unfounded assumption here—is that they've never needed such a word because they don't see themselves as separate from the world around them in the way we do. Or maybe people who haven't been coddled like we have with the double-edged blessings of civilization can't afford to see themselves as separate. If they're going to survive, they have to live as part of the world, not apart from it.

There's an Inuktitut word, "isangajuq," which perhaps illustrates this lack of separateness. *Isangajuq*, I'm told, can mean three different things: a human with arms flung wide, a bird with wings outstretched, and the stars spread out across the night sky. As for the elusive term you're searching for, I came across another useful word while I was in the Arctic, *nuannaarpoq*, which means something like "taking pleasure in the awareness of being alive."

See you soon,
James

New York, USA
December 2 1981

Dear James,

Do you remember the first letter you wrote to me? The note you left at the front desk of the hotel in Iceland? My plane was leaving early in the morning and you wanted to let me know what you'd learned about the wild orchids of the island, and about the frogs living near the hot springs. And there were some other things you wanted to tell me, too.

So now it's my turn. It's almost midnight and I'm writing this in the lobby of your hotel so that you'll find it waiting for you at the front desk when you check out in the morning.

After Nancy's reception I went home and tried to sleep. That proved impossible, with what had happened between us tonight. The kiss we shared when we said goodnight was so brief but it said so many things that both of us have never been able to say. It was magical but for me it was also terrifying, and I want to explain why, if I can.

After lying awake and realizing sleep just wasn't going to happen I called a cab and drove across town to your hotel. I was going to have the desk clerk phone up to your room just now, but something kept me from doing it, even though I had the feeling that you weren't sleeping either. Instead I'm going to finish this note and then go back to my hotel again. Maybe that makes me a coward, but when I got here and started walking toward the front desk I felt like a child taking her first tottering steps. I knew I just wasn't ready for what might happen if I asked the clerk to make that call to your room.

It's been hectic for me as the chief organizer of the festivities. People want to help, and sometimes they really do, but just as often they're only getting in the way. Anyhow, once again you and I didn't really get much time together, just the two of us, I mean. So I didn't get around to saying some of the things I meant to, about how much I admire and respect you, the work you do and the outlook you have on life. You've changed my own way of seeing things and helped me through the darkest time in my life. I'm so grateful for that, and I think a lot about us becoming closer, how good it would be, but I'm frightened too and I don't know what to say or do when you're near me. It's only a short time since I had any feeling at all but emptiness. After what I've lost it's as if I can't believe the world or fate or life will allow me to be happy. Or maybe I'm terrified that if I dare open my heart it will only be broken again.

I have to go. I don't know who I am tonight. All I know for sure is that these days I'm prone to sudden attacks of irrational worry for people I care about. The thought of the long journey you're making is weighing on me.

Please take care of yourself in Antarctica. Keep warm and come home safely.

Love,
Martha

McMurdo Station, Antarctica
December 9 1981

Dear Martha,

You're right, I wasn't asleep when you came to the hotel. I was awake, thinking about you. In the morning I read your note when I came down to the lobby and I looked around and then ran out the door looking for your cab, hoping absurdly that you hadn't driven away yet. I read the note again in the shuttle on the way to the airport, and in the waiting lounge, and on the plane. I have it with me now and I keep looking at it as if I can't believe it's really there.

You said you were terrified by what happened between us and the truth is I share that feeling. I know there's no way I can really understand what you've suffered and how you feel. And that's made me keep my distance because I was afraid if I told you how I felt I would only hurt you. And then lose you. I want us to be closer too, but it has to be what you want.

I had a lot of time to think on the plane, and for now I'm just going to concentrate on the work ahead. Our Hercules transport left Christchurch, New Zealand in total darkness that slowly paled as we drew further south. Looking out the plane window I could see icebergs begin to appear like ghosts in the black waves far below, and then suddenly there was a band of radiance ahead of us that grew and grew, as if Antarctica was the source of all the world's light.

We arrived at the station in the middle of the night and the sun was still high up in a dazzling turquoise sky. The only sign of cloud was a long, thin, white plume of steam trailing out from Mt Erebus, the active volcano that looms over McMurdo Sound.

When we landed the other researchers and I stepped gingerly, like astronauts, onto the frozen runway. The pure frigid Antarctic air shot into our lungs like liquid nitrogen. We trudged in a daze to the station, were shown our quarters and stowed away our gear. Then we gathered for a quick meal that was either a late dinner or an early breakfast, looking numbly around us as if we were in a dream. We are, really. A dream that for most of us was a long time in being realized.

I've been here three days now and have come to see that McMurdo is a weird, vigorous hybrid between a wild frontier town and a military base. The US Navy pretty much runs the show here, which explains why people call the dining hall the "galley" and the bathroom the "head." But things are complicated by the presence of so many seasonal researchers, engineers, mechanics, and other part-time visitors. They are climatologists, ecologists, hydrologists, you name it, all of them speaking their own specialized lingo. There is a team here hoping to find dinosaur fossils in order to prove the great lizards lived on this continent, too. A lot of the personnel, both scientists and others, are gung-ho young guys for whom Antarctica is the perfect place to prove how macho they are. Consequently there is a fair bit of hard drinking, hazing of fresh "earthlings" and a code of ethics you might find at a construction site. Toughness, pulling your weight, getting the job done, that's the culture here. Unfortunately so is talking to and about women as if they're either weaklings or the entertainment.

On the positive side, thriftiness is sacred at McMurdo, I shouldn't forget that. Don't waste anything. Use the minimum. Wash your dishes in an inch of water and rinse them the same way. This might be a good way for the rest of us to learn to use our planet's precious resources before we're forced to it by necessity.

The temperature today at noon was a balmy 3 degrees celsius (that's about 37 above for you non-metric folks). It generally dips down to minus 10 at "night" during the summer here. Not too bad at all—much like Vancouver in winter, except that the air is bone-dry.

Today I took a walking tour of the area around the station. This place is old enough to have gathered some historical landmarks, like the "Discovery Hut," Robert Falcon Scott's base camp. The first church built in Antarctica is here, as well as several monuments that commemorate people who have died at the station over the years. The most recent such memorial is for a Navy man who was killed just last February in a cargo-loading accident. I climbed Observation Hill, a steep volcanic knoll that gives a panoramic view of McMurdo Sound and the Transantarctic Mountains. There isn't much here to obstruct the view, of course. Other than the weather. On the way up the hill I passed a group of buildings that I found out later used to be a nuclear power plant. It was shut down in the early '70's when faults were found in the structure. A nuclear power generator in a volcanic zone? I don't understand it either.

This afternoon the clouds rolled in and there's a forecast of snow. I'm scheduled for helicopter transport to the Dry Valleys tomorrow if the weather cooperates. At this season, with new people arriving for the summer, there are planes that take outgoing mail, so I'm taking advantage of that to write you this letter before I head off on my research trip.

What you said in your letter, and the way you brought it to me, means a great deal. If I still have a hopeful outlook on life it has a lot to do with you. So far I've been keeping warm, and I do plan to get home safe and sound.

With love,
James

Lake Heimdall Research Camp, Antarctica
February 12 1982

Dear Martha,

The day after tomorrow I'll be returning from the Dry Valleys and a few days later I will be leaving Antarctica, so you'll probably get this letter after I'm already back home.

My expedition to the Valleys was delayed for over a week by bad weather. I spent a lot of time cooped up at McMurdo, playing cards, chatting with people and looking out the window at the blowing snow, thinking that I was never going to get to carry out my research.

I talked a lot with a climatologist from Columbia University who's been studying the fluctuations of the Antarctic ice sheet. His name is James, too, although he insisted I call him Jim. He stunned me with dire predictions about what might happen should the industrial world continue to pump ever more heat-trapping carbon dioxide into the atmosphere. I have to say I was skeptical at first of the doomsday scenarios he spun for me. The polar ice sheets entirely melting and the sea rising hundreds of feet and monster hurricanes a regular occurrence rather than a once-in-a-century event.... Most of the scientists I've talked to about climate are worried about just the opposite: what humanity can do to survive the next ice age, which is due any time now, geologically speaking. But as Jim patiently laid out for me the mechanisms of climate change, a field I don't claim to have any expertise in, what he was saying began to sound a lot more credible.

"I've talked to people in industry and the government about this," Jim said with a lot of frustration in his voice, " and most of them think I'm a crackpot. They think I'm dreaming up the next Charlton Heston disaster flick."

Finally the weather cleared enough that the helicopter was allowed to leave. It was still quite foggy on the way to the Valleys, but once we arrived at the research camp, the strong winds had blown away all the cloud cover, and the sky, like the earth itself, was dazzling and pristine.

The winds and the shielding mountains are what make the Dry Valleys the geological oddity they are. This is the only place in the Antarctic that is free of ice, so that you can actually walk on and study the soil of this continent. There has been next to no snowfall here as long as records have been kept, and the last time it rained was two million years ago, which is what my Dad would say about Saskatchewan.

Now I understand why they call them dry. My eyes are red and stinging, my lips cracked like glacier crevasses. These polar desert valleys are comparable in stark lifeless aridity to the surface of Mars. The breathtaking beauty of this landscape is the beauty of absolutes. Remember how barren Iceland seemed, how we agreed it was like standing on the moon? Iceland is an English garden compared to this place. This is why scientists have been scrambling to get out here for years now. There is much to be learned about life on earth and the possibility of life elsewhere in the universe from a place of extremes like this, where a few living organisms persist and thrive in the teeth of the killing forces of nature. In this terrain change is so slow as to be almost undetectable to human observation. A ham sandwich dropped here will still be here millennia from now, pretty much intact if not edible, long after our civilization has passed on the torch to another—and if we truly learn what Antarctica has to teach, chances are better that there will be someone to pass this knowledge on to.

Heimdall Lake camp is a two-room quonset structure and a couple of outlying storage sheds. The walls rattle in the wind and there's frost on the insides of the windows every morning. At present I'm sharing this luxury wilderness resort with three other researchers, two Americans and an Austrian, all good folk. Living here for any length of time, one of them said to me, is a bit like being on board a ship. Your freedom of movement is constrained in a similar way and there's also a corresponding necessity to keep the day occupied and structured with tasks, not only for the sake of survival, but also to help ward off the gradual psychic erosion that such a place can cause. I don't know if I'll be here long enough for that to affect me. So far I've spent each day like a kid in a gigantic candy store, wandering among the rocks and stones.

I hike out every morning in light clothing—"light" for this place that is, although I do bring along extra layers for wind protection if need be. I carry a radio, a lunch, a water flask, my notebook, and a urine bottle (yes that has to be carried back out too). Titanic glaciers flank the sides of the valley like vast half-ruined monuments from the ancient world. At the far end of the valley stand three jagged, pyramidal peaks: the Matterhorn, the Anti-Matterhorn, and the Whassamatterhorn (why are scientist jokes always so awful?). Here and there you come across pinnacles of rock that have been scoured and sculpted by the ferocious winds into grotesque and comical shapes. Down by the lakeshore I found the mummified carcasses of seals that somehow took a wrong turn at the coast and wandered inland to their death. Some of these carcasses, I'm told, are thousands of years old. Nobody knows what causes these poor creatures to make such an error in navigation, or having made it, to persist in it against the obvious. Well, maybe humans aren't so different in that respect.

I can't forget to mention the stars. With no light pollution here from cities at night, there are more stars than I'd ever imagined one could see with the naked eye.

And yes I found what I came to find. Cryptoendoliths. After I'd finished my research I was tempted to take one of these small, inconspicuous stones with me, to give to you, but in the end I decided you would agree with me that they should stay right here where they've been getting along perfectly fine for ages.

I have many more Antarctic tales to tell you but I'll save them for when we meet again, which I hope will be soon.

With love,
James

New York, USA
March 6 1982

Dear James,

Your letters from the South Pole arrived today, both of
them on the same day. The first one must have gone astray
for a while at Penguin Post. And thank you again for taking
the time to call me right after you returned. I'm glad that
you accomplished everything you set out to do, but it was
also a great relief to know you were back home safe and
sound.

I had a strange encounter in Greenwich Village the
other day (no surprise there, I suppose). I was eating lunch
in a little deli when a woman walked by outside with a
llama on a leash. Of course, this being a typical noisy New
York lunch hour, it took a second or two before my brain,
on its usual shut-out-the-world mode, grasped what I was
seeing. By the time I got out onto the street both llama and
llama-woman had vanished. I laughed out loud. Here I had
just been thinking about you and then something strange
happened.

I pushed my way through the crowd and luckily
caught sight of woman-with-llama about to turn a corner,
so I hurried after them. I remembered your talk with that
man named Jerry on the library steps, and how there was a
time I used to chase after stories like this. And I knew both
you and Nancy would never forgive me if I didn't.

The llama-woman's name, or as much of her name as
she would give me, is Ronnie. She looked to be about fifty

years old, though she may be younger. Her face was severe and weathered and none too clean. She wasn't particularly easy to talk to—her conversation jumped all over the place and I suspect she has some kind of mental illness, which is often the reason people end up homeless in the first place. She told me she bought the llama from a farm near Danbury, Connecticut. She was quite specific about the location, as if she didn't want me to think she'd stolen it. I have heard that more and more people are breeding llamas, and that some people here in the States actually use them as pack animals for long hiking trips.

Anyhow, the llama's name is Kisco, which sounded to me like an Inca word but apparently it's the name of Ronnie's hometown. Kisco really is a gorgeous animal. His coat is a beautiful black and white patchwork, making it seem a bit like he's wearing a mask and a tuxedo. Very dapper and sophisticated, for a llama. Ronnie and Kisco live in a beat-up old motorhome, it turns out—something like your van, perhaps!—and when Ronnie gets together enough money for gas they move on, driving up and down the east coast. From some things she said I got the feeling Ronnie does have a family, or relatives, who help her out from time to time—she was wearing expensive running shoes that looked almost brand-new, for one thing. And I detected a trace of Boston brahmin in her speech and manner, too, e.g., when she told me she'd been with Kisco for "about three yee-ahs." I was reminded of my old literature prof in college, who used to proclaim with incontrovertible authority that "*thee* greatest *nawv*elist in the English language is of *coss* Jane *Awe*sten."

I offered to buy them both lunch—Ronnie a sandwich and Kisco some carrots, if I could find some, but I could see Ronnie was starting to chafe at all my questions. She kept glancing around as if looking for an escape route, and then she said, "Kisco wants to get going now. He doesn't like staying in one place long."

I didn't want to let them go. There was a story here and for the first time in a long time I was excited about it. Maybe the opening piece for the book. I asked her if there was anything at all I could do for her, and she got angry.

"Why would I need you to do something for me?" she snapped at me.

"Well, I just thought…"

"Where's your man, huh? Where's your big handsome man? Why are you eating alone?"

That stopped me cold.

"Why would you ask me that?" I snapped back, getting annoyed now.

She cackled at me.

"Yeah, what business is it of mine. Nosy, nosy me. Hah. So you just go and mind your own darn business, missy."

Well, fair enough. I'd come on too strong. So I just wished Ronnie well and watched her and Kisco vanish into the crowd. Had to smile though about being called "missy."

Love,
Martha

P.S. The cryptoendolith by the way is doing fine, at least as far as I can tell. I've always felt more responsible for this little band of green than I do for any of the other plants I've tried to nurture. Perhaps it's because of something you once told me, that these tiny forms of life can go into suspended animation and revive years later. This is something I think I can understand. I haven't gone out to inspect my garden plot for a couple of years now. I think I will soon.

Love,
Martha

Vancouver, Canada
March 12 1982

Dear Martha,

Thank you for the story of Ronnie and Kisco. You're right—you'd have been in trouble with Nancy and me if you'd let that one get by.

Right after I got back to Vancouver I had to fly to a conference in Calgary, so I feel like I haven't quite arrived home yet. I'm on leave from teaching this year, but buried in all the work that has to be done to get my data into shape. And when that's done I have to go see my dad. It has been far too long since I've spent any time with him. He tells me there's a new woman in his life, and he wants me to meet her. He thinks this one might finally be a keeper. That was the word he used: "keeper." It's so strange, for the first time in my life I've got this protective feeling about him, as if I have to go make sure this woman is right for the old man. Usually my first impulse with his new girlfriends is to warn *them*! But Dad's talking about his latest romance in a different way. Quieter. More serious. So we shall see. Anyhow, as if there isn't enough to do, I'm also already preparing for another trip that's been in the works for a while, a return to Indonesia to follow up on the research I did there back in the 70's.

I'm hoping to visit you again soon and tell you all about my travels, but I'm not sure when that will be.

Love,
James

New York, USA
March 19 1982

Dear James,

As much as I would love to have you visit, I understand you're busy and I'm glad that you're going to see your father. One should never wait to make those visits. You never know if you'll get another opportunity.

Nancy has been gone only a few months now, and just as you said once, things have gotten a little quieter but also a lot less interesting. I always knew I relied on her, but I never realized how much until she wasn't there to fall back on.

I've started working in my garden again. I neglected it for a long time, and expected someone might have taken over the space while I was absent, but the only thing I found when I went back was bare soil and a single star-shaped white flower that I couldn't identify. Mom came to the garden with me last weekend and she knew what the lovely blossom was right away—a wood anemone, a wildflower that must have gotten here on its own initiative. Mom has more herbal lore at her fingertips than I'll ever know. The anemone is a springtime flower, and it won't last, of course, but it has brought me something valuable. When I first saw it I said a silent thank you for something so lovely. I haven't let the beauty of the world in like that for a very long time.

Love,
Martha

St Ives, England
April 16 1982

Hey Jimbo,

A belated thank you again for being part of my wedding day and for the cedar box of sand from Jericho Beach. Truly a perfect gift. I should've written sooner but hey, you were in Antarctica and I was busy trying out my brand-new husband.

Tony and I are on our delayed honeymoon now in sunny tropical Cornwall. Brrr. It's Tony's native ground, otherwise I'd be on the next train outtahere.

I think you'd like these people, James. One of Tony's uncles is the local expert on the history of tin mining and another is only too happy to tell you all about Cornwall's many interesting species of freshwater molluscs. And here I thought the British were boring know-it-alls. What larks, Pip!

I called Martha the other night and she told me all about your adventures at the South Pole and how you've barely gotten home and now you're planning another expedition this summer to Indonesia. Excuse me, but isn't there something else you should be doing? Namely getting on a plane to the city that's so nice they named it twice.

This may come as a shock to you but I figured out a long time ago who your "mystery woman" was. Duh. I think it was when I got to thinking about two people who kept on writing letters back and forth for years about bugs and rocks and elephant droppings. Yeah right. And there was that time you kept insisting "I'm a bachelor," like the word had some hidden meaning. So I finally looked it up in the dictionary and found this: "bachelor, n., a male bird or mammal without a mate, esp. one prevented from breeding by a dominant male." And the lightbulb flicked on. Thanks for the hint.

So anyhow, yeah sure the letter-writing is kind of romantic, but it's also a way of keeping someone at a distance isn't it? Someone who you're not allowed to have those feelings for that you're having.

With my keen eye and discerning mind I observed what was going on between the two of you during my wedding. Believe me that nothing would make me happier than to see it continue to go on (is that grammatical?) but now I hear from a reliable source that the two of you are back at opposite ends of the continent writing letters again. James, as your official pain in the rear, I tell you that this will not do.

A long time ago you and I learned that some things are not meant to be. And maybe that's because other things are. You've always been a puzzle to me, but I'm guessing you're worried that you want this more than Martha really does, that you don't want to hurt her, that if you take that irrevocable step it will be the wrong moment. I also think that deep down inside, the tidy bachelor is scared to death that his safe, solitary kingdom is coming to an end. And maybe the scientist is worried, too, that he doesn't have enough data to be certain he's doing the right thing.

I can't tell you what will happen the next time you and Martha see each other but I know this: if you wait until something is a dead certainty, by that time it may just be dead.

And you were wrong. You should eat the swans.

God it's cold here. Tony is warm and furry—my very own Tom Jones—but I'm still glad I brought one of my grandmother's quilts.

Ch-ch-ch-cheers,
Nancy

Vancouver, Canada
April 30, 1982

Dear Nancy,

You're right.

James

Somewhere in South Dakota, USA
May 2 1982

Dear Martha,

I'm writing this at an RV campground a few miles outside the town of Rapid City. My trusty old van is parked nearby, looking dustier than usual and a little dazed to find itself in a place it didn't expect to be. Like its owner. It isn't quite motorhome season yet, and there's only one other vehicle at the campground, a tent trailer occupied by a young couple who haven't spent much time outside of it. They've been serenading me with their enthusiasm all evening.

I won't be mailing this letter, since I'm hoping to deliver it in person. In which case maybe I don't even need to write it. But I will anyway. I need to do something other than just sit here by myself wishing I was with you.

On my way back from visiting my Dad in Saskatchewan I stopped at a place called Chinook Valley, a couple of hours drive north of Vancouver—and yes, I met his new girlfriend, Dora. She is a very nice lady, and she bakes a mean saskatoon pie.

I always keep camping and hiking gear with me when I travel, in case of these sudden longings for solitude. In my part of the world there are some fabled places tucked away here and there, like Chinook Valley, which has gained an almost mythical status among ecologists and other nature-loving types. For some reason I'd never made it up there before. It is said that funny things happen in this valley to compasses and watches, and that anyone who spends time in this remote little stretch of wilderness feels a mystical sense of harmony and wellbeing.

These past days I've been thinking even more than I usually do about you. About what it is I truly want my life to be. To be for. It occurred to me this would be a good place to hide out from work and travel plans for a while and think these things through, if I can. Probably *thinking* too much.

I drove as far as I could along a narrow forestry road and came to a small settlement and hunting lodge hacked out of the bush, where one of the last of the hunters and trappers, a man named Al Olafson, gave me directions for the rest of the journey in. This involved hiking up a high pass and down the other side into a marsh swarming with ravenous mosquitoes. As for the valley's reputation for oddness, Al had only this to say: "People bring it with them."

Itchy, damp, and footsore, I finally reached Chinook Creek a few miles from where it flows into Cache Lake (I'm telling you these names in the strictest confidence, of course. I don't want someone building a golf course here). As per Al's instructions I hiked another few kilometres to the far end of the lake, where it was less boggy and there were fewer bugs, and set up my one-man pup tent in a meadow that sloped down to the rocky shore. It was already pretty late by this time, so I didn't bother with a fire, I just ate a meal of cold pea soup from a can, slung my food supplies on a rope between two trees and went to bed. Happy to report my sleep was undisturbed.

For the next couple of days until my food ran out I stayed put. In the mornings I watched the sun's light redden the snowy tops of the mountains. They reminded me of the strawberry-flavoured ice cones my dad used to buy me at the summer fair in our hometown on the prairie. I watched the mist drift off from the lake. I hiked around the shoreline and inspected the mosses and lichens. I saw signs of moose and bear and came face to face with a coyote who grinned at me like he'd never seen anything so ridiculous and then loped nonchalantly off into the woods.

I caught up on my reading—I had Shakespeare with me again as well as a wise letter from Nancy—made some entries in my journal, and for a lot of the time just sat by the lake and let my thoughts go where they would. I remembered what the Musketeer had said to me that night on the Amazon. I shouted at the lake: "What is it I don't see?" and then I felt foolish as my melodramatic echo came bouncing back to me across the water. After that I just sat on the shore and let the sun and cloud shadows pass over me.

Then I discovered I wasn't the only would-be hermit out here. On the afternoon of the third day I spotted a small fire on the far shore of the lake. My first thought was *Damn him!* I wondered if he had heard my idiotic shouting. My binoculars showed me a youngish-looking man sitting in front of the fire cooking something in a pot. I saw his shiny new red nylon tent and his shiny new red nylon backpack. I'm still lugging around the heavy canvas stuff I bought years ago. The other fellow was bearded and pretty shaggy-looking, but beyond that I couldn't make out his features. At one point he glanced up and stared in my direction. I don't know how well he could see me from that distance but I felt like I'd been caught spying so I put the binoculars away.

That evening I sat in front of the campfire looking up at the stars, then I went down to the lake. The yellow moon was just rising over a flat-topped ridge. It seemed to be nested there like the golden egg of some fabulous bird. The other solitary camper had a fire going too. I could see him move in front of its light from time to time.

The surface of the lake was calm and still in the moonlight. Somehow I knew that the guy on the far shore was sitting there watching the lake too. Or watching me. About an hour went by. My fire dimmed then lit back up then dimmed again. His did the same. It was as if our campfires were having the conversation we weren't. Finally they sank down to coals and didn't light up again. Silence. Then out of the water a fish leapt. Probably a lake trout. I don't really know. There it was, a flash of silver in the moonlight, and the next moment it was gone, with a faint splash that echoed and swiftly faded away.

I sat in front of the fire until it died down to the last glowworm embers. Then I climbed into my tent and went to sleep. After I don't know how long I was woken up by the sound of shouting. I stuck my head out of the tent. The fire, as often happens, had hunkered down until it found a little more fuel and now it was burning brightly again. So was *his*. I couldn't see him but he was out there somewhere, growling and cursing and weeping, and with the firelight dancing the shadows of the trees around me and that noise coming across the water I felt a little unnerved. His voice sounded louder than I would have expected from that distance, as if he were somewhere not so far away, wandering around in the woods. I couldn't catch everything he was bellowing but I heard "There are a million stars out here" and then "They'll be the only witnesses." I'm guessing he was either high on something or this was some poor paranoid soul who had come up here to wrestle with his demons. Or both.

So much for a mystical sense of harmony and well-being.

Strange to say, I didn't feel threatened. I listened to him and it struck me that the wilderness really is an unsatisfying place to go wild. You stamp and scream and throw rocks and sticks, you shake your fist at the universe, and nothing around you notices or cares in the least.

I waited until the fire died again and then I got back into my sleeping bag and listened to the shouting as it grew more intermittent and fainter. At some point I drifted off to sleep. When I got up the next morning, pleased to find myself still alive, I checked with the binoculars and saw that the other guy's campsite was deserted. No bright red nylon to be seen. That night there was no fire across the lake. My friend had apparently packed up and left. Back to his job as an elementary school teacher. Or an ecologist. Who knows.

I hiked back to the settlement the next morning to find Al Olafson smoking a pipe on his rickety porch, looking like he was waiting for me. I was going to tell him what happened, and ask if he knew of anyone else who'd gone up to the lake, but then I remembered what he'd said about how "people bring it with them." So I just bought him a beer at the hunting lodge and then got in my van and headed for home. My compass and watch, by the way, performed the entire time with their usual reliability.

I drove for three hours on the forestry road, trying without success to pick up a station on the van's antediluvian radio. Playing the same Gordon Lightfoot albums over and over on my crummy old eight-track. Then, as dusk was closing in, I reached the junction with the highway south to Vancouver. For another hour I drove on the highway, keeping myself awake with the grating, twangy country music that the radio finally managed to pluck out of the ether. Every once in a long while a car would pass going the other way, and each time this happened the truth kept tugging at me, that I was going in the wrong direction.

Finally I pulled over to the side of the road and got out of the van. I remembered the madman at the lake, and I thought that in some way I really had brought him with me. I mean that he was showing me what I was in danger of turning into if I let my life go on as it has for so long. Either that or it would be time to find a llama and hit the road. I thought of you, of course, and how you came to my hotel on an impulse the night before I left for Antarctica. I thought of the things I've wanted to tell you for a long time, but have never had the courage to say, or even write. Then I got back in the van, turned around, and headed back up the highway, away from home.

I found a secondary road south that eventually, after a few wrong turns, took me south of the border. At one point I ended up on a winding forestry road that took me to the bare top of a mountain. I got out of the van again and stood there in the wind and the dark, looking for lights or some landmark that might tell me where I was. The voice of prudence said: *maybe some force is at work here to keep you from going through with this crazy idea.* Then I thought about Jerry on highway 63, deciding to finally face his fear. And I thought, prudence is a dear old gal, I've known her for a lot of years and she's rarely steered me wrong. But this time I didn't listen to her. I got back in the van and retraced my route until I found a main road. It was already quite late by this time, so I pulled over to sleep at a campground near the town of Kettle Falls, Washington.

A thought just now: this impulse took me over once before, the day I set out walking and ended up at Point Roberts. I just didn't admit to myself then where I really wanted to go.

Today I drove quite a good distance, through all of Montana, the northeast corner of Wyoming, and into South Dakota. I was on the road for at least fifteen hours, with a couple of short breaks in some of the most loneliest little towns I've ever seen. Tomorrow, if my sense of distance and geography isn't too out of touch with reality, I should make it to Chicago. I don't know what the following day will bring, but it will finish this trip and begin something I can't see the end of. As terrifying as this is, that's how it should be.

James

Dover, New Jersey, USA
May 4 1982

Dear Martha,

I'm groggy, unshaven, my hair sticking up all over, and the inside of my van looks like a landfill. The traffic has been increasing steadily the further east I go. The night before last I spent in the town of Berwyn, Illinois—where the heck am I?—driving around a suburban maze until two in the morning. Last night as I tried to sleep a highway kept on rolling endlessly before me in my head. I've checked into a motel tonight so I can have a shower and sleep in a decent bed. Tomorrow morning I'm going to pay a visit to the nearest shopping mall (it just occurred to me that I don't have any clean clothes) and then drive the last few miles into New York City. That is, if my nerve doesn't fail me and I turn around and scurry home with my tail between my legs.

Did you know that a hedgehog's heart beats over three hundred times per minute?

James

New York, USA
May 5 1982

Dear Nancy,

Sincere thanks for your untiring work as my official pain in the butt. I took your sage advice and ran with it. Or rather, drove with it. Three thousand miles or so. The last leg of the journey was completed by bus, since that indefatigable workhorse, my trusty old "Nir-Van-a," finally gave up the unleaded ghost just outside Jersey City. I guess I'm stranded in Manhattan for the foreseeable future but that's just fine. Things are, as you put it, continuing to go on.

Martha sends her love.

Your friend,
James

New York, USA
May 6 1982

Dear Nancy,

As you know from James' letter, he arrived here yesterday. We have been together every moment since. James forgot, though, to include a little-known fact in his letter, so I am doing that for him.

I wonder if you've ever heard of the bonobo, a close relative of the chimpanzee. It's the only primate, other than humans, that engages in sex simply for pleasure and companionship. Bonobos have been observed stopping for a little whoopee at all times of day, and in the midst of other tasks. They certainly know how to seize the moment.

Love,
Martha

London, England
May 17 1982

Dear both of you guys,

This is good. Very good. SUPER GOOD! For once in my
life I'm at a loss for words.

LOVE LOVE LOVE,
Nancy

3

Magelang, Indonesia
June 12, 1983

My love,

I'm nearing the end of my research, in record time, and I'll
be heading home in a couple of weeks. Sooner, if I can get
everything done on schedule. Which is rare, but I'm trying.
I can't wait to be with you again.

You're on my mind wherever I go. Your face, your touch, your voice. It's all I can do not to grab the next flight out of here. Writing this letter to you will have to do until it's finally time to come home.

Yesterday was the total solar eclipse over this part of the world. I watched it from a hilltop overlooking the sea. I've always been annoyed at myself for missing the total eclipse over Oregon and the Canadian prairies in '79. Too busy at work then to bother making the trip!

The place is called Borobudur, site of the world's largest Buddhist temple complex. Even without an eclipse this place is incredible. It was built some time in the eighth century and abandoned about a hundred years later as a result of increased volcanic activity, which eventually buried the site. It wasn't until the nineteenth century that Borobudur was rediscovered, by a British expedition led by Sir Thomas Raffles (who lent his name to the world's largest flower, Rafflesia, which bursts into full bloom only in the middle of the night, during the rain). Over the past ten years, with the support of UNESCO, the temple has been restored, and finally, this year, it was opened to the public.

By the time I arrived the temple grounds were already swarming with people singing and laughing and chattering in a dozen languages. Hawkers selling and buying food and t-shirts and pieces of smoked glass. It looked and sounded and smelled like a carnival. Well, it was, really.

I attached myself to a guided tour and found out that the temple has three levels, each one corresponding to a plane in the Buddhist cosmos:

Kamadhatu, the lowest level, is that of human passions. It is also known as the world of illusion, according to our tour guide (she was a young woman who smiled a lot at one member of our group, a handsome young man.)

Ruphadhatu is a level of ornamented terraces that depict in stone the life of Prince Siddhartha Gautama, who became the Buddha.

Arupadhatu, the highest level, is that of abstraction and freedom from human desire. We didn't stay long at this height.

Pilgrims walk around the entire structure from the bottom to the large stupa at the summit, to symbolize the journey from illusion toward enlightenment.

At one point the guide gave a short talk on the life of the Buddha. I don't know how much historical truth there is in what she told us. Still, it makes for a beautiful story and she was a terrific storyteller. Unlike me, but I'm going to try to tell it like she did.

It starts with a king who's told by a seer that his newborn son will either grow up to be a mighty conqueror or the saviour of humanity. The king is appalled. *Saviour?* No son of his is going to waste his time *saving* people. This child will rule after him, carry on the family name, win glory, subjugate empires. The world will bow before him.

So the king keeps his son Siddhartha enclosed in a palace of delights and wonders. Happy and safe from contact with the miserable, disease-ridden poor and their problems. And from any of those wandering holy fools who would put ridiculous ideas of God and religion into his head. Here in the palace his son will know only hunting, feasting, music, games, dancing girls. The proper pleasures of kings.

And so it is. Siddhartha grows to young manhood in his father's palace, never seeing the outside world, never learning about pain and sorrow and death. Then one day his curiosity about what lies beyond the gilded walls finally gets the better of him. With the help of a loyal servant, Siddhartha slips unseen out of the palace. He finally enters the city his father rules, the city he will one day rule.

There he meets a homeless beggar. He's never seen such a thing, a man all covered in dirt and sores, his clothes nothing but grimy rags. Shocked and sickened he walks on unseeing and stumbles over a sick woman huddled by the side of the road. She's hacking and shivering and moaning in pain. He's still looking back at that horrifying sight and nearly runs into a frail man hobbling along on a stick, his face seamed with wrinkles, his eyes clouded, his toothless mouth gaping open. What's wrong with *him*? The prince has never before met anyone who is *old.*

Further on a group of weeping men and women are carrying someone lying on a litter down to the river's edge. Siddhartha's servant explains that this is a dead body being taken to be burned on a pyre. *A dead body?* What can that mean?

The prince moves closer. The mourners, terrified at the sight of this noble figure adorned with jewels, set down the litter and grovel in the dust. The prince bends over the figure they were carrying. A beautiful young girl, her skin grey, her body stiff and lifeless.

What is this? Siddhartha asks, confused and angry. *What's happened to her?* The servant explains that this is the way life is for human beings. We suffer because we are born, we get sick, we grow old, and finally we die. The fragile spark of life goes out of us. Unless it is fed to the fire the body that remains will begin to smell and rot and be eaten by worms.

The servant gestures to a heap of bones lying in a mound of ashes near the water's edge. This is all that remains of a human being after death has eaten everything else. *This is what death looks like, my lord. This is how it is for everyone.*

Not for me, the prince says in horror. *This will not happen to me. My father won't let it.*

The servant is afraid to contradict his master and so he agrees.

It is as you say, my lord, the servant murmurs. *This will not happen to you.*

But Siddhartha can see the fear in the man's eyes. He demands the truth.

Yes, it's true, the terrified servant admits at last. *All this will happen to you, too, my lord. Some day you will fall ill. One day you will grow old. And one day you will die and become a heap of bones.*

And so the prince discovers suffering. He hurries back to his palace of pleasures, but all he can think of is what he's learned today. All of these horrors will be visited upon to him, too. He can't escape. No one can. And now the happy days and nights of music and feasting and lovemaking are poisoned. Pleasures no longer please, not even the small, insignificant ones, because he sees at last that every joy ends. Nothing *stays*. So you grasp after another pleasure, another distraction, and it ends, too, and leaves you unsatisfied, hungry, seeking yet another temporary escape from the pain of things changing and ending. You can spend your life running and hiding from sickness, from the bent back and feeble limbs of old age, from that heap of bones beside the river, but they will always find you.

No. There must be a way to escape this fate. There must be. Siddhartha is determined to find it. He will defeat these age-old enemies of humankind (maybe this is the "mighty conqueror" showing up in him). So he leaves. Says a tearful farewell to his young wife and his infant son and walks out of the pleasure palace, into the world of beggars and the sick and the dying. Somewhere there must be a cure for human suffering, and he will be the one who brings it to the world. He will not stop, he will not give in, until he finds the answer.

For six long years he searches. He meets holy fools and sages, learns from them the arts of meditation, of stilling the mind and looking within. He nearly starves himself to death believing he must renounce even the body's most primal needs in order to find wisdom.

Then one day he just stops. He renounces even renouncing. He's walking along a river and then he just stops and sits down in the cool shade of a tree. Rests his feet. A girl looking after cows nearby notices this half-dead holy man and brings him a bowl of rice and milk. Siddhartha takes it gratefully and eats. Once he has restored himself he vows not to move from this spot until he finds what he seeks.

So he sits there under that tree by the river. This was the part of the story I could relate to, of course. Sitting in the forest, waiting for something to happen.

Days go by. The girl returns each morning with a bowl of milk and rice. Siddhartha eats. He sits. Barely moving. Just breathing. Then one night, just before dawn, he looks up and sees the morning star, and it happens. He awakens. He is the Buddha.

He has found the answer.

That's where the guide ended her story. She just smiled and walked on to the next part of the tour, like the "answer" was already known to everyone. I'd heard about the Buddha's enlightenment before, but I never gave it much thought. Guess I assumed it was just another fairy tale, like the ones they used to tell at church back home in Saskatchewan. But the story hooked me, strangely enough. I really wanted to know what the Buddha had found. I wanted her to state it in terms anyone could relate to and understand. What did it mean that he'd "awakened"? What had changed? But other people in the tour group were already asking her questions about this and that, as if they knew the rest of the story, too. I felt like the only one not in on the secret. So I never asked my question.

Later I watched the busy eager people around me, fussing with their fancy optical instruments and grumbling about the heat, all of us so fixated on what was going to happen, impatient for it to happen, annoyed at having to wait so long for it to happen. And I thought there really was a lot of truth in the Buddha's understanding of human unhappiness. Anyway I still have to ask myself if it matters at all, what the Buddha found. We have each other, and it's good, and all I want is just to share this happiness with you.

I ran into an Australian botanist I'd met at a conference in Melbourne a few years back. He invited me to join his party, who were setting out for a nearby hilltop where they hoped there'd be a less noisy and impeded viewing of the eclipse. Sweating and grunting, we hauled all of our equipment up the hill in the heat. Welding glasses, stopwatches, temperature and humidity gauges, cameras, all of this paraphernalia. For a couple of hours before the eclipse was scheduled to begin we watched birds through binoculars to see if they exhibited any strange behaviour. Someone brought a caged canary he had bought in the nearby village of Magelang, where I'm writing this now. Someone else had his golden retriever with him, a beautiful, friendly dog named Bailey whom everyone took turns petting and playing with.

Then someone shouted for our attention: it was about to begin. We took up our welding glasses and no one made a sound, except for Bailey the dog, who had been unimpressed by all the noise but was now whining and circling her owner, who finally managed to calm her down.

As it turned out, the call for attention was a bit early. We began to fidget as the seconds ticked by and nothing happened. I sat down again and started drowsing off in the heat. Daydreaming. Then someone gasped and it was like we all woke up, just like that. People shouting *here it is, here it is!* and we all looked up and the moon, which had vanished in the glare as it climbed toward the sun, was suddenly there again: a grey notch on the white-hot solar disc.

Between that moment of "first contact" and totality almost an hour went by, but the little group on the hill remained alert, watchful, apprehensive the entire time. It occurred to me we were like a collection of solitary planets, all turned toward the centre of our universe, held in thrall, unable to tear ourselves away.

Totality approached at last and a deep, rich shade of indigo fell over the earth. Then the grey shadow of the moon was suddenly gone and a black disc appeared in the sky. Of course we knew it was the moon, but this blackness was not at all like the shadow we'd been watching. It was like a hole had opened in the universe. A hole into absolute nothingness. People gasped and shouted and screamed. I heard a man weeping.

A chill sank in. It was night, and not night. A corona burst out all around the black disc. Blazing, full of colours. So intensely bright that even with the welding goggles I could hardly bear it. In some directions the sun sent off streamers that seemed to extend for millions of miles into space.

Everything fell away. I don't know how else to say it. For a long instant, a timeless time, everything, myself included, was lost. Was gone. Had never been. I felt as if the last time I had seen you was a thousand years ago, in another life.

Then, thankfully, the sun came back, and the ordinary world after it. It started as a sudden stab of light at the edge of the black disc, and then there was no more black disc to be seen, just a fiery crescent that grew back into the sun we remembered and loved and were so thankful to see again. We set aside our goggles and looked at one another, blinking and staring like bats woken up in the middle of day. My hands were shaking. Bailey was barking her head off. People cheered and sang. There was a weird greenish glow behind the hills to the northeast, as if another, unknown planet was about to rise.

Everyone started jumping around like kids and whooping in excitement, working off all the fear and adrenalin. People I didn't know were slapping me on the back like old friends. I just stood there. I couldn't move. Something had become completely real for me that had always just been an idea, an intellectual truth that had never really touched me. For the first time I felt it in my bones, that I was standing on the surface of this vast sphere spinning and hurtling through space. And then all I could think about was that you're on the other side.

It's raining here now, great thundering torrents turning the street outside the hotel into a river. I've been pacing the room like a caged animal. What am I doing in this place? The thought that you'll be there when I get home is almost driving me mad.

All my love,
James

New York, USA
June 18, 1983

Dearest James,

I can't wait to see you again. I'm happy for you, that you finally got to see a full eclipse. I wish I'd been there to share it. Now I just want you back.

It has been a busy, hectic time the past couple of weeks. Mom is moved in now with Aunt Tess and that seems to be going well. Two strong-willed women in the same apartment—it'll take a while for them both to adjust. Mom knew how I was feeling about leaving her to move so far away. She came right out and told me not to worry about it. She also admitted she's wanted to move in with her sister for a long time but felt she couldn't because the cottage meant so much to me. It still does, of course, but we've had to face financial reality.

And on that subject, it looks like the sale will go through okay. Philip has been very helpful with the realtors and lawyers and paperwork, and more importantly, he and I had the chance for a long-overdue talk that I think was good for both of us. He and his wife Ellen are expecting their first baby in December. I wish them all the best.

When most of our belongings were packed up I had one last night at the cottage by myself. The preparations for moving have kept me so busy I haven't had time to really accept that I'm leaving this place. I went down to the shore in the evening, where I'd found the injured gull, and where Michael and I spent that magical evening. I looked out at the waves and the feeling I'd been pushing away for so long finally got past my defenses.

All of sudden I remembered a night when I was working late on something and Michael came to my room. He was supposed to be in bed asleep, but of course it always took several tries before he thought we really meant it. Philip was out for the evening with friends and I was deep into the writing, and this was probably the third or fourth time Michael had gotten out of bed since I'd tucked him in and said goodnight. I slammed my pen down and herded him back to his bedroom, barely listening to his excited chatter. He had dug a flashlight out of a cupboard, and he wanted to show me something amazing he had discovered.

"Look Mommy," he said, "I'm full of light."

I looked at his hand, glowing a deep mysterious red where he held it over the flashlight lens. His fingers like glass. Fragile, newly-blown glass, still hot from the fire.

This was a marvelous discovery to him, but of course I'd seen this little trick many times before, I'd done the same thing as a kid, so I just muttered something like "okay, that's nice, now go to sleep," and tucked him under his covers and hurried back to my work.

Remembering this all these years later caused me such pain that I had to stop walking. I couldn't even stand up. I dropped down right there in the surf. The grief had returned so powerfully, James, that I thought I might die. I wanted to die. I wanted the waves to come in and just take me. If there's an afterlife where I get to be with my little boy, then just take me so that I can be with him again. If there isn't, then at least there won't be this pain anymore, and the both of us, Michael and I, will be at peace.

It will be so much harder than I ever imagined, leaving this place. I hope you'll understand. I know it's foolish but I feel I'm leaving my child behind. I've been telling myself, and him, that it's not true, that he'll always be with me, that we'll always be together. But some part of me, a deeper, stronger part, believes I'm abandoning him. Forgetting him.

I left the next morning and spent the night with Mom and Aunt Tess in the city. Yesterday morning I went for a walk in Central Park. I crossed Bow Bridge, where Michael and I used to stand and look out over the water on our daily outings together. In the Sheep Meadow I took off my shoes and socks and walked through the grass barefoot. As I was approaching the lake the sun reached down into the park and lit everything up as if it was all brand new: the lawns, the walkways, the trees.

It was morning but there were already lots of people at the lake: families, young couples, old couples. I sat down on a bench next to a middle-aged white woman in a long brown robe. Her head was shaved and I looked at her and thought to myself that she had to be a Buddhist monk, or nun, or something like that. It made me think of the story you heard at Borobudur, about the Buddha's life. How you never got the chance to ask what the Buddha found, what the answer was to life's suffering.

So I asked her.

Well, not quite like that. Here's how it went:

I said, "Excuse me, I hope this isn't rude, but are you a Buddhist ... um ... monk?"

She laughed this beautiful bright laugh that made me like her immediately.

"I'm so glad you asked that," she said. "Those boys there (she pointed to a nearby family with young kids feeding the ducks) came running over here a minute ago and asked me if I was a Jedi knight."

It was my turn to laugh, and then we chatted for a while. Her name is Reverend Mizu Edmonds ("Mizu" is her Japanese ordination name—she's a Zen monk, not nun—who lives in northern England). I learned a little about her monastic order, how it was started by one of the first Japanese masters to emigrate to England to teach meditation. She'd come to New York with a contingent of her fellow British monks for some sort of Buddhist conclave. The temple they were meeting at was not far from the park, and she was just taking a breather from the proceedings. That reminded her she had to be on her way soon, and she got up to go. I thought *this is my chance.* I told her why I'd asked her if she was a monk: I was hoping she could tell me the rest of the story, what the Buddha found under that tree, so that I could tell my husband, who'd just heard the story told and wanted to understand the ending.

"What the Buddha *found?*" she asked, as if she wasn't sure what I meant.

"That's right," I said. "When he sat under that tree and looked up at the morning star. What happened? What did he see?"

"Well," she said, "I suppose he saw the morning star."

There was a twinkle in her eye and I knew she knew what I was really asking. Or at least I think she did. Maybe I don't know what I was really asking.

"It's a beautiful story, isn't it?" she said. "It's like a fairy tale run backwards. Instead of a penniless young man setting out into the world and ending up a prince, the hero is a prince at the beginning and gives all his riches away, all the things that most stories are about *getting,* to seek something else."

"It is beautiful," I said, determined not to give up, "but the *something else* part... I mean, if you had to put it into just a few words..."

She laughed.

"You mean can I give you a sound bite to take away with you?"

"Well, I suppose so. Yes."

She took a deep breath.

"Hmm, let's see," she said. "I could tell you that when he saw the morning star the Buddha realized his true nature. But that wouldn't help much, would it?"

"Not really."

"How about this. The Buddha realized he was, is, and will be enlightened with all beings."

"Umm..."

She laughed again.

"Didn't think so. You know, when you asked me the question my first impulse was to say that the Buddha discovered he was not alone. That doesn't seem very profound, I suppose, but it's what I want to tell you. What the Buddha knew, *really knew* for the first time, was that he was not alone."

I thanked her, but to tell the truth I was disappointed. I'd taken a real liking to this woman, and then she hands me this trite new age slogan. I hope I didn't let my feelings show. Anyhow, we talked for a while longer and she wished me the best for my new life in Canada, and I wished her the best with her conference and trip home, and we parted.

I walked around the park for a while longer, thinking about what she'd said. It occurred to me that the real reason I'd asked her about the Buddha's story was not just to report back to you but because I wanted the end of the story too. I was asking for myself. I wanted some truth that would make the suffering end.

So then I was ashamed of myself. How could the pain ever go away unless I forgot Michael. Is that what I wanted? Did I *want* to forget my little boy? I turned around and went back to the lake to look for Reverend Mizu, hoping she was still there so I could tell her how I was really feeling. Tell her the truth, that I am alone. I know this will hurt you to hear, James, but it's true. Despite being in love with a man who loves me, part of me will always be alone because my little boy is gone. What would the Buddha say to that, I wanted to ask her. Had *he* ever lost someone he loved more than life itself?

But of course she was gone. So I walked back to Mom's place. We had coffee and talked about all sorts of things, going over old family stories. I was thinking about you the whole time and wishing you were here.

Be safe, and hurry home!
Love,
Martha

Reykjavik, Iceland
June 26 1985

Dear Nancy,

I've been so caught up with getting my book finished, it was good to put all that aside and spend time with you and Tony again after so long. Thanks again for letting us invade your lovely home.

When we got to Dundee James and I went looking for the house I'd lived in as a child. Thanks to Mom's still-phenomenal memory we found it. We knocked timidly on the door and waited. A middle-aged woman answered. She seemed a bit suspicious at first, but after we'd explained ourselves, she warmed right up and gave us an extended tour.

As we went through the house all of these forgotten memories came flooding back. I remembered the way the light came down the dark narrow hall from the little back passage window. I remembered baking bread with my mother in the little, high-ceilinged kitchen, and the corner my father sat in when he read his newspaper, how I liked to crawl up on the shoulder of his chair, and how we had this game where I would pluck carefully at the hairs at the back of his head, and he would talk about pesky mice and pretend he didn't know it was me. I spotted a dent in the hardwood floor of the front parlor and   remembered it came from when the movers were taking out Mom's piano and let it drop once a little on the way. Piano not damaged, but Mom livid. And I remembered how, when everyone else went outside to say goodbye to the neighbors I stayed inside and lay down on the cool floor and put my finger in the dent. I don't know why.

Mom had asked me to inquire after her old friend Mrs Brody, who looked after me sometimes when I was small. The woman, Margaret, had only lived in the house a short time, but she knew who we meant, and she took us up the street to introduce us to her. Mrs Brody was frail and hard of hearing, but she said she remembered my mother and me very well. She recalled one time when I was over at her house, and I was sitting at the window, singing something to myself, and when she asked me what I was singing, I stuck my nose in the air and said, like the little smart-aleck I was, "A song."

From Scotland James and I flew to Reykjavik, almost ten years to the day since either of us had been there. Yesterday we went on an excursion to the geysers, where we first met and talked all those years ago. It was definitely warmer then. While we were standing there huddled together, waiting for nature to put on its show, James admitted something that had me speechless with disbelief. In his very first letter to me, he'd mentioned that Iceland had a small population of frogs, escapees from a school biology class. He told me a story back then about how they sometimes get blown into the air by geysers.

Now he tells me this was a lie. The scrupulous, fact-loving scientist lied to me! He says that he didn't think there was anything interesting about him so he decided to jazz up the letter with something really astounding. It had to be memorable so I wouldn't fold it away and not bother to write back. He swears that to the best of his knowledge he's never misrepresented nature since.

I'll forgive him, eventually. Do you know how many people I passed on that curious and little-known "fact" to over the years? The frogs of Iceland. I can't believe I fell for that. But now I have the story to open my book with.

Love,
Martha

P.S. A strange fact of my own, but true: I've had a hankering on this trip for the unlikeliest foods. I even tried haggis in Scotland, God help me. And something the Icelanders call surmjolkurlaup. Yummy stuff, but don't ask me to pronounce that.

I wonder what could be causing these odd cravings?

Vancouver, Canada
January 15 1986

Dear Martha,

Living in the same house, we haven't needed to exchange letters for a long time, but it feels right to put pen to paper again.

Watching you give birth to our son was the most terrifying and moving experience of my life. Every time you had a contraction, the strain brought lines out in your forehead and at the corners of your eyes that faded away again when the pressure lessened. I could see, in your face, what the word *labour* truly means. And then, as soon as he was out and on your breast it was as if all of that pain and stress had never been. You looked so truly and profoundly happy. Darwin talked about "endless forms most beautiful and most wonderful." After all of the places I've visited and the amazing things I've seen, I had no idea that the most wondrous sight of all was still waiting for me.

Love,
James

Vancouver, Canada
January 15 1986

Dear James,

I've been trying to come up with a title for the book, and now I have it: *Endless Forms Most Wonderful*. Thank you for that.

And you're supposed to be the expert on biology, so you should count yourself as part of this new wonder. I couldn't have done it without you.

Love forever,
Martha

4

Chris W.

Dear Mom,
Happy birthday! This is my drawing of a frog. Dad told me you liked them.
love, Chris

Vancouver, Canada
January 4 1998

Dear Nancy,

Chris and Emma love the gifts. Thank you! We missed you so much over the holidays. It has become a real tradition for Christmas to have Aunt Nancy and Uncle Tony with us, but of course they understand you can't be here every year. It's long-overdue to be our turn to visit you. I'm hoping it will be next year. As you know last year was busy for us with James retiring early from teaching and research in order to involve himself more fully in local environmental issues. This was supposed to make life a little less hectic around here, but I think in fact it did the opposite. Maybe next Christmas, as you've been hinting, we'll send Chris to visit you on his own, if I can work up the courage to let him fly all the way across the Atlantic by himself.

In the meantime, it looks like this year it'll be my turn to travel. I've been invited to join an international group of journalists and photographers on a tour of "the changing face of China." No family allowed on the trip, unfortunately.

As the kids have grown and started asking questions about their heritage, I've had a stronger desire than ever to learn more of my family history. Taking Chris and Emma to Scotland last year was a worthwhile and rewarding experience but I still feel there are so many things I don't know, especially about China. Like me, Mom remembers very little about the place she was born. And it's not likely she'll ever have the chance to revisit it, as I did Scotland, to see if she can recover some of what has been lost.

I know this has a lot to do with our grandfather, about this strange feeling I've always had that it was my duty or destiny to find out what had happened to him. I know that I can't do that, at least in the sense of tangible evidence, documents and such. I simply want to be there for a while, keep my mind and senses open to see what I can learn from the feel of the place. The sky, the land, the people.

So James will be staying home with the kids while I am gone. Chris is eleven now and Emma is seven, but I still feel a lot of anxiety about leaving them. This will be the first time I've been apart from them for more than a day or two.

Love to you and Tony from all of us,
Martha

London, England
January 17 1998

Dearest Cuz,

You're going to China at last—I'm so thrilled for you! And no, it isn't your job to find out what happened to Grandpa or anyone. Just bring yourself back, please. That's all I ask and I'm sure James and the kids say the same.

And yes, yes, yes. I want you to send my favorite nephew in the whole world here next Christmas. And then the year after that, if you're ready, it can be my favorite niece's turn!

Love ya
Nancy

Beijing, People's Republic of China
May 6 1998

Dear Chris and Emma,

Hello sweethearts! Miss you so much! I arrived yesterday in the morning and I had a bad case of jet lag, so that I felt like sleeping during the day and staying awake all night. A bit like you two, come to think of it. But I am feeling a lot better today and have spent the day sightseeing.

Beijing is an amazing city. Even being from New York I can't quite believe the crowds in the streets. The people, especially the young people, dress mostly in familiar western styles, although grunge hasn't caught on here yet. Or maybe it already came and went.

You're going to like this story. After breakfast we headed down Wangfujing Street, Beijing's famous outdoor pedestrian mall, just me and two other female journalists. This was our first real taste of the new China, the dare-I-say-it capitalist China, and there was no shortage of friendly young people who were happy to talk to us about their favorite shops and what clothes they wore and what music they liked. In fact there were so many intriguing stores and stalls that after a while the journalistic expedition turned into a full-on shopping spree.

I was looking for gifts for everyone at home and lost sight of the others. Then I shook myself out of my bargain-hunting haze and realized I wasn't on Wangfujing Street anymore: this was some narrow side street and I had no idea which way to go to get back to our hotel. I went over to a parked cab and asked the driver if he could take me to Wangfujing Street. I thought I was pronouncing the name of the street properly, but he couldn't understand me. He just shrugged his shoulders and spoke in Chinese. I got angry at the poor man and walked away, and that's when I realized how famished I was. Breakfast had been hours ago. I figured I'd better eat something before I set out to find my way home. Didn't want to faint in the middle of this crowded street.

I walked along for a while and finally found a restaurant with plastic strips hanging in the entryway instead of a door (somehow that's how I knew for sure it was a restaurant, even though I've never seen a doorway like that before). The frontage didn't look promising, but this was no time to be choosy. I ducked in through the flaps and found myself in a small steamy room jam-packed with Chinese people in workers' overalls slurping noodles. Just like in a cowboy movie everyone in the place stopped what they were doing and turned to stare stone-faced at the stranger in town. And the stranger lost her nerve. She did! The gutsy journalist turned tail and fled.

I'm writing this now in a McDonald's. Yes, that's right. I'm embarrassed to say how relieved I was to catch sight of those familiar golden arches. Like an oasis in the desert. I haven't eaten at a McDonald's in decades but here I sit gobbling oversalted French fries and slurping a milkshake. At least the clerk at the counter looked at my map and showed me how to get back to the hotel. So all's well that end's well. Let's hope!

I miss you so much. *Zaijian.*

Love,
Mom

Beijing, People's Republic of China
May 8 1998

Dear James,

I've been faithfully keeping my journal and snapping photos, so there will be lots to tell you when I return, but with the free time I have in the evenings I thought it would be good to write to you as well. I don't do well alone in hotel rooms, and writing, as always, helps. I've been feeling a little overwhelmed, to be honest, what with the exotic foods, the crowds in the streets, even the unfamiliar smell of the air. Culture shock has definitely kicked in. While our little troupe of journalists is together during the day we have a great time, meeting people, exploring, discussing the surprising or disconcerting things we're seeing. And then everybody says goodnight and retreats to their own rooms and it gets quiet. Too quiet. That's when I start thinking about how far away from home I am.

It's the middle of the night right now, actually. I woke up an hour ago (4:30 AM) from a dream that I was back home with you and the kids, and in the pitch dark I didn't know where on earth I was. You weren't beside me. I called out for you, then remembered I was thousands of miles from home. I got up and I looked out the window and saw only blackness. It seems they turn off most of the lights in this city after dark, perhaps to save on energy costs. Looking out into the dark I had a moment of irrational panic. About being so far from home, from you and the kids. About what might happen without me being there to do anything about it. Don't worry, just starting this letter has already helped the fear pass. I will be fine.

We have been assigned two official guide/interpreters. The head guide is Mr Li, a former army officer who is unfailingly considerate and professional but who insists on strict punctuality, like a drill sergeant. His assistant is Ms Xiao, a gentle, lovely young woman who has adopted a western first name, June. Since learning that we are both mothers (she has a son who is nine), June and I have become fast friends. I stick close to her most of the time because I've noticed I don't always get the most welcoming glances in the streets, at least from men. Women are a different story—the ones we have met are endlessly curious about me and my life at home in Canada. I have been asked countless times "are you married?" and "how many children do you have?" I've also been asked to pose for a photo with almost everyone I've been introduced to, which is flattering of course for a woman of a certain age.

Yesterday our indispensable guides took us to visit Chairman Mao's Mausoleum and the Forbidden City, and today we went to see the Great Wall at a place called Badaling. Our meetings with Chinese officials and journalists begin tomorrow, and I suspect the schedule was set up this way deliberately, so that we'd first be brought to a state of intimidated awe at the vast splendor of China's history and culture before we talk to anyone official. Maybe that's cynical, but yesterday I was in Tiananmen Square and it was sobering to stand there and think about what happened in this place less than ten years ago. The celebrations of the students, their youthful hope for change and freedom, and the brutal crushing of that hope under the wheels of tanks.

The line-up to pay respects to the remains of the Chairman stretched all the way around the massive building he's housed in, but it moved constantly, so that one never had the sense of getting nowhere. I have to say I wasn't there with a lot of respect in mind. Maybe just to say I'd been there, done that. And I wasn't the only one. Behind me in line a British tourist muttered to his wife "Why do we build these monuments to mass murderers?" and the wife whispered back "For the love of God Kenneth do you want to get us arrested?"

At the entrance, where people were presenting flowers before a disconcertingly Lincoln-like statue of Mao, there was a rather peremptory sign in English: "Please remove all hats and keep quiet." The Chairman, or a reasonable facsimile thereof, lies in a glass coffin, inside a room also walled off with glass. Something didn't seem quite real about him—his face had a kind of plastic glow, like one of those snowmen you see in front yards at Christmastime with a lightbulb in them. I really question whether this is the real Mao or just a wax dummy.

The Forbidden City is immense, and takes a long time to traverse from one end to the other. Despite the crowds of sightseers, though, it seemed empty, in a monumental kind of way. Vast courtyards with high walls that shut out any view of the modern city. Mr. Li pointed out a Buddhist inscription above a door which roughly translates as "Do nothing." Isn't that wonderful? Nobody in this country seems to be following that advice, though.

The Great Wall surprised me by being, well, a wall. Not that it isn't incredible to see how it threads its way over mountaintops and into gorges. But the fact that it's here at all says a lot about the emperors who had it built. How does a ruler who has conquered territory after territory, kingdom after kingdom, protect everything that now belongs to him alone? Put a wall around it! Like the "Keep Out" sign Chris has on his bedroom door. A child's idea of security, when you think about it, and kind of sad and funny at the same time. Though the suffering and death involved in the wall's construction is anything but. History proves again and again that whenever someone powerful gets a Big Idea, people are likely to die.

I've been trying to dig up fascinating facts about nature here. One problem is that China, at least the populous areas, doesn't seem to have a lot of what we think of as nature left anymore. Even on the way to the Great Wall, passing through countryside, I hardly saw a bird or anything more exotic than a water buffalo pulling a plow. Which is pretty exotic, granted, coming from the other side of the world, but the sight of man and beast plowing a field (with electrical transmission towers in the distance) seems more a postcard-style image of China than a real experience of nature. The air is quite dirty and acrid here, as well, much more so even than in New York, tangibly so. Yesterday, after a long day of sightseeing, my eyes were sore and stinging. Today at the Great Wall I looked up and saw a clear blue sky, and realized that I hadn't seen that at all in Beijing.

Wo aì ni,
Martha
(I'll tell you what that means when I get home)

Xi'an, People's Republic of China
May 12 1998

Dear James,

I miss you and Chris and Emma more than I can say. I have to ask you, James, please don't share this letter with the kids. Maybe someday I can show it to them, but what I have to tell you, what happened to me here, would be too painful for them, I think, and hard for them to understand. You'll see what I mean when you get further into the letter.

I am now in Shaanxi Province, the ancient heartland of Chinese civilization. This was not on our itinerary before we arrived. Not the first time we've found our daily schedule changed at the last minute without any reason being offered by our hosts. Mr Li just marshals us together with no explanation, as if this new activity was always the plan for the day. But I was thrilled when I found out we were going here— as you know I've wanted to see the terracotta warriors ever since I first read about their discovery all those years ago.

We took a private bus from the airport to the city just as dusk was falling. There were bonfires burning on the roadside, and dust and smoke obscured the sunset. The long drive through shadowy, crowded streets became more and more dreamlike, and I had the odd feeling we were going back in time, entering a mysterious city of long ago.

At a stoplight a young family on a motorcycle pulled up beside us. The man was driving, and between him and his wife sat a little girl. They were talking as they waited at the light, and the little girl first leaned against her mother and then her father. It took me by surprise, this moment of quiet tenderness in the middle of a crowded street. We've always heard in the west that girls aren't as valued here as boys are. That's not what I saw then. Another "fact" complicated by experience.

When we got to our hotel, our hosts in Xi'an took us out for a late dinner and some celebratory cups of rice wine. Everyone was exhausted, and one by one we westerners excused ourselves, but you'll be amazed to hear I stayed to the end, drinking and chatting with people I barely knew.

The rice wine helped Mr Li loosen up a little and stop playing the drill sergeant. He began singing some Mongolian folk songs he'd learned in his years up north with the army. What a surprise: he could really belt out a tune. A few of our hosts soon joined in. Then everyone, Mr Li and June and the Xi'an people, all began singing a slower song that struck me with its beauty, even though I couldn't understand the words. Some of the people had tears in their eyes. June explained that it was a traditional love song, well-known and beloved all over China. She translated part of it for me:

> Horses running in the mountains.
> In the dark sky a white cloud.
> The moon shines bright over Kangding town.
>
> The woodcutter's beautiful daughter.
> The eldest son of Zhang has come to court her
> in the moonlight.

What was that Inuit word you once told me about? The word that means taking pleasure in being alive. As I listened to the singing I said to myself *Yes, I'm alive. Right here, now. This is life.* It wasn't a particularly joyful feeling, or a sad one, for that matter. Or maybe it was both and everything in between. But I didn't want to rush away from it, like I usually do. So I stayed and listened to the singing. At one point they tried to teach me the lyrics to one of the songs, so I could sing along. Everyone, including me, laughed at my bungled attempts to pronounce the Chinese words properly. June put her arm around me, this spontaneous gesture of affection I hadn't expected. It moved me deeply.

The next day we drove by bus to the site of the warriors. The building we pulled up at was disappointingly nondescript and run-down looking, like a great big warehouse. It turned out they've got things set up so that you have to walk through the gift shop to get to the actual museum, which is much more dignified and impressive. In one corner of the shop, surrounded by tacky souvenirs, sat an old man at a table. A sign identified him as the farmer who dug up the first evidence of this forgotten burial ground in 1974. June says the first thing he found was the clay head of a general, which he stuck on a pole to scare off the crows.

The warriors are kept in a vast vaulted room, easily three times the length of an Olympic swimming pool. We walked through another door to get into this great hall, and then suddenly, there they were. Column after column of silent, earthen figures, some with limbs and heads missing, some with arms outstretched to hold long-crumbled-away spears and swords. As you know, each face is unique, but to actually see this was something else—both delightful and spooky at the same time.

According to legend the emperor Shi Huangdi was so obsessed with the thought of his own mortality that he decreed six thousand living soldiers were to be killed on the day he died, to serve him as a suitably imperial entourage in the afterlife. His ministers talked him out of this cold-blooded plan by tactfully suggesting that if word got to the army about this plan it would incite a revolt. The idea of the clay warriors was quickly dreamed up by a quick-thinking advisor, as a less bloody alternative.

We moved slowly along the rows of these silent figures, looking into their unseeing eyes. I don't know if I can convey how moving this place is. The warriors were never living men, but being among them is like standing in the presence of the dead. The long dead.

In one area of the hall the excavation of a burial chamber was only half-finished. I saw a clay standard-bearer buried up to his shoulders, leaning his head against the side of the pit, as if he was just resting before continuing to pull himself up out of the earth. I remembered the story you heard in Indonesia, how the Buddha discovered the causes of suffering, and the first of them was simply being born. I was suddenly just so sad. For all of us. And so full of love, too.

I thought of when Chris was little, how he came to our room at night crying because of all his unanswered, unanswerable questions about life and death. I thought of Emma, how difficult her birth was and how beautiful she was when she finally made it, spiked-up red hair and all. I thought of you, James, and what we've accomplished together, and how precious each moment of life is.

Then I thought about Michael and how sad it has always seemed to me that the three of you never met him, never knew him, although I see him in our children every day. I remembered a dream I'd had long ago, when I was a girl, about China. There was a little boy in that dream, playing in a garden. We played together, and then he had to go. At the time I thought this was my grandfather. I'd been hoping that visiting China would help me to understand him better, but now I think that little boy wasn't him.

This evening, after we got back to the hotel and ate dinner, we visited a lovely wooded park, one of the few that has survived from ancient times. In the middle of the park, amid a grove of white pines (I made a point of confirming the species, James) was a small ornamental lake spanned by a graceful, arching bridge of white stone that reminded me a lot of Bow Bridge in Central Park. We walked out onto the bridge in the moonlight, and it was so peaceful and that alabaster bridge was so radiant over the dark water, it was like walking on a beam of light across the night sky.

Mr Li tells us the names of everything we see, but he was having trouble with this particular translation, so June gave it a try. She said that the bridge's name was like the word for rainbow, but a rainbow made by moonlight. I think they were startled when I laughed and said they didn't need to translate. I knew what the name was, because my husband had seen one of these years ago, at sea. This had to be Moonbow Bridge. Well, then I had to explain to June about our letters to each other, our love of rare and unusual facts. And that got me thinking about home again, and all of you.

We all went back to the hotel and said our goodnights. I was hoping for a restful night's sleep after a long day, but it wouldn't come. Something was bothering me, biting at me. I suppose it was partly that same sense of being so far from my family that I'd been feeling mostly in the evenings, but it was more than that, too, or something else. It was like a physical pain more than anything, but one that I couldn't quite locate in the body. Finally I got up, got dressed, and went downstairs to the lobby. The desk clerk stared at me like I was some kind of apparition. He actually came out from behind the desk to ask me if I needed help. I told him I was going for a walk, and he looked terrified and tried to talk me out of it. Said it wasn't a good idea.

"Robbers?" I asked, pointing my finger like a gun.

He waved his hands.

"No, China very safe. No robbers."

"Well what's the problem then?"

He had no answer to that and I felt bad because I sensed he was afraid that if I got into trouble so would he. But I went out anyway. I walked back to the park, to the grove of trees and the pond, and onto Moonbow Bridge. It had been raining earlier and the bridge deck was wet and shining.

I stood there for a while, still feeling restless and anxious. Angry, too. The anger just kept growing, without any reason or source. As if I was being held against my will in the grip of something I couldn't see. It didn't get better or go away out here in the peaceful park, in fact it got worse. I looked out at the still dark water, the shadows under the trees, the few stars in the sky, and I felt nothing for any of it. It was like I was sealed away from everything around me in an invisible prison. Or I was the prison, caging something in.

This is nothing, I said to myself. *All of this is nothing.*

Then it became unbearable, this anger and anguish. It boiled up into a despairing rage that was like a hot blade through my heart. I'd never felt anything like this before, not even in the terrible days after Michael died. Why was this happening to me now? You have a good life, I told myself. You have more love and joy in your life than so many people ever get in this world. But still it took me over, this rage and pain, until that's all there was.

For some reason then the prayer of Saint Patrick came into my head. I sank down onto the stones and I spoke the words aloud, barely able to choke them out: *Stand with me against every cruel, merciless power that may oppose my body and my soul.* I didn't even know who I was asking for help, if anyone. And then I felt there was no one to stand with me. I was praying to no one and no one was listening.

Where is this power? I shouted into the dark like a fool. *Where are you? Show yourself. Show yourself or just destroy me. End this.*

I heard something then and turned. A young couple, holding hands, had been walking toward the bridge, but they'd stopped when they heard my shouting. They looked at me with something like terror, then they turned around and started walking quickly away.

They were afraid of the crazy white woman on the bridge and I didn't blame them. They'd probably been looking forward to sharing the bridge and the moonlight with each other, and all I'd accomplished with my insane outburst was to ruin their romantic evening.

I thought about what they must have seen when they looked at me, and all of a sudden I understood who my enemy was. I saw for the first time that the cruel, merciless power in my own life was not whatever had taken my child from me, not fate or chance or God. It was *me*, punishing myself. Pushing away joy because I didn't believe I deserved to be happy.

The tears came and I let them come. Then I got up and crossed to the far side of the bridge, not really knowing what I was doing. All I could think of was that I should find that young couple and apologize to them, or at least show them, if we couldn't speak to one another, that the bridge was theirs now if they wanted it.

I roamed around the park for a while and discovered that it was much larger than I had assumed. I couldn't find the young couple, which was just as well for them, I suppose, given the state I was in. Just like in Beijing I managed to get lost for a while, but eventually, I found my way back to the bridge. It was deserted. I crossed to the middle again and stood looking at the water, with a different feeling now. A trembling, expectant feeling, that something was about to be revealed to me.

I stood there until the sun came up, a fiery blaze pouring out from the space between two office towers. A narrow band of light flooded into the park. I looked and I saw every leaf and every blade of grass glowing from within, alive with its own small fire. Just like Michael holding up the flashlight to his fingers that day.

And something happened. Something changed in things, or in me. Or both. It was like my head came up out of murky water into light and air. Dark water that I'd been in for so long I took it for the way things really are. But now there was nothing between me and anything else, and everything was shining. And I heard, clear as day, my little boy saying, "Look, Mommy."

He was there, James. As real as I was.

For so long the beauty of the world only hurt. It reminded me that Michael was no longer here to share it with. But now, for the first time since I lost him, I could feel him with me. I knew, I *know* in the depths of my being that he is here, asking me to look, to really look and see him in every good and beautiful thing.

Reverend Mizu had it right. I'm not alone. No one is.

I know you don't look for spiritual experiences in nature, James, but you've mentioned in the past that you listen to things, waiting for them to speak to you. I didn't know I'd been waiting for Michael to speak to me this way. Or perhaps I forgot how to listen, or was afraid to. But I've gotten the message now. I've listened and I've seen what it was he was trying to show me that night, with the flashlight held up to his hand. I know now that I can leave this place and he will be with me, always. And I've seen and I know that beneath everything we fear and desire, beneath everything we believe we are or have to be, there is nothing but peace and joy.

I stood in the middle of that bridge and I saw my life, both the past and what is to come, like a slender, gleaming span stretching out over the dark water. And at either end were the people I love.

I am with you all, now and forever.

Epilogue

June 7 2004

My love,

Evening is falling, and Emma and Chris and I are sitting by the lake in Central Park. It's the last day of our visit to the city you once called home.

I brought a journal with me on this trip, something I haven't done for a while. Glancing back I see that the most recent entry is dated over a year ago. It has been that long since I last set down my thoughts and experiences—something that I used to do every day without fail. It has been that long, I suppose, since I've seen or felt the wonder in things and wanted to preserve it in words. And thinking about that, I realize how long it has been since I wrote you a letter.

We have had a full four days, and I think they have been very good for this family. On the afternoon we landed and checked into the hotel, the kids dragged me straight back out into the streets to have a look around. Chris and Emma were full of pent-up energy after the long flight. They wanted to see everything famous right away. I think for a while they forgot the real purpose of our visit, and I was pleased about that. I was glad to see them simply enjoying themselves, excited by something new and different for the first time in a long while. I knew the next couple of days would be difficult enough.

On our first full day here we went first to Ground Zero. It's a construction zone now, while plans are being made for a memorial and for the Freedom Tower that will rise here. We talked about our memories of 9-11, how we all gathered at home that day to watch events unfold on television, how we wept together at the horror and the darkness that had fallen over the world and struck so close to home.

We didn't stay long at the site. Emma, with her sensitive nature, found it overwhelming. And I felt wrong about being there somehow—that we were tourists who had come to gawk at tragedy and take photos.

Next we visited the Natural History Museum. We found the Haida canoe, with its solemn, stiff mannequins. Lifeless images of our attempt to understand a world that we can never really know. We made our way through gallery after gallery of mysteries and marvels to the geology hall, and I had a little chat with Peary's meteorite, to the great embarrassment of our offspring.

Later, we got lost for a while in the jungle of the upper west side, but finally found the building you had lived in. Whoever has the apartment now wasn't home when we rang the bell. Probably for the best. Who knows how they would have reacted to us three footsore wayfarers.

We admired the ginkgo trees that we found along some of the streets, and stopped by the old community garden, which is still flourishing despite pressure from developers. In the afternoon we went to the Bronx Zoo, and made a special point of visiting the giraffes. In the evening we went back to the hotel and I called Nancy and thanked her for sending me the letters that you and I wrote to her over the years. Now I have the whole story gathered together, something that Chris and Emma can read when they're ready.

On our second day I fulfilled the promise I made to you one year ago, to visit Michael on his birthday, like you used to do. In the morning we rented a car and drove out to your mother's old house on Long Island. Philip came from the city and met us for lunch, then took us to the cemetery on the hill where Michael is buried. Emma and Chris hardly said a word when we visited the gravesite. Over the years they've heard a lot about Michael from you, and they've always been curious about him, but in a distant kind of way, as if to them he has never seemed quite real. I think again, as I have many times before, how strange it is that they never met their half-brother. I know it must be difficult for them to spend time with me — it's been so long since we've really been together, the three of us. I think, though, that they understand this is one of the reasons we're here.

Before we left the gravesite Emma turned to me.

"Do you believe they're together?" she asked. "Michael and Mom?"

I was going to give her the answer she wanted to hear, to comfort her, but instead, I told her how I really felt. The scientist's answer. And maybe that's why the kids have never asked me anything like this before.

"I just don't know, sweetheart," I told her. "I'd like to think they are."

"Mom believed they would be, didn't she?"

"Your mother didn't believe. She knew."

Both Emma and Chris looked like they wanted to hear more, but they didn't say anything. Instead we just walked out of the cemetery in silence. I knew there was a better answer to Emma's question, an answer that took you many years to find. I'd brought that answer with me, in my backpack, for just this moment, and I knew now was the time to begin sharing it with them.

We found a place for a picnic, on a sandy slope covered in sparse tufts of Indian grass, overlooking the sea. The pine barrens weren't far off, and I thought I could catch just the faintest, almost secretive scent of resin in the hot midday air. You told me once that it was the last patch of wilderness on the island.

I took out the letters you and I wrote to each other over the years and began reading them to the kids. Or at least I tried to. When I couldn't keep my voice steady Emma took the letters and read them for me. We didn't get through all of them that afternoon. None of us wanted to rush this. We cried at some of what we read, and laughed at a lot of it. More laughing than crying, all told. It was good.

The kids and I saved the park for our last full day in the city. It's a big place and we didn't want to rush this either. We started in the morning and roamed from one end to the other, taking our time, getting sidetracked, not bothering with maps or signposts. As we walked, we talked about some of what we'd read in the letters, about what this place had meant to you.

We wandered through thick woods. We clambered over boulders, hopped across streams. We sat for a while in the shade of a little grove of Scots pines that reminded me almost painfully of home, so much so that the kids had to talk me out of trying to climb one of the trees for old time's sake. Coming around a leafy corner we were surprised by a bronze sculpture of a mountain lion, crouched on a rock, ready to spring. We stood on Bow Bridge for a long time, looking at the water. We toured Shakespeare's garden and watched a troupe of actors put on a silent performance of Romeo and Juliet. You'd think Shakespeare with the words taken out would defeat the point, but it was a powerful experience watching these timeless characters drawn to their sad fate in silence, yearning but unable to speak those familiar phrases. Chris, I think, was especially taken with it. His interest in acting as a possible life path has been growing, although he's still very much into saving the whales and the idea of a career in marine biology.

We ate lunch at Tavern on the Green and later stumbled across Strawberry Fields, the place where people leave flowers and tributes to John Lennon. They've apparently got flowers here from almost all the countries of the world. Chris wondered if there was a good place to leave flowers for you, and I thought about it for a moment, and then the answer came to me. The perfect spot.

You've been gone for almost a year now, and it has been very hard. Chris and Emma and I haven't always been as close and "together" as we were today. I've been so angry for so long, until it became almost unconscious, like breathing. It was either that, I think, or simply give in to the emptiness. You told me one night at the hospital that you had come to understand what your life had been for, and this was a great comfort to you, but I couldn't see that then, or didn't want to, and I still haven't accepted it, if I ever will. It is not fair, it is not right that you were taken from us so soon, and I don't know that I will ever make peace with that.

When it came to the kids I felt powerless to help them, and I withdrew into myself for far too long. I lost the most important knowledge, you could say, the knowledge of who I really am, and I woke up one day, not long ago, and I saw that because of this I was in danger of losing them, too.

Of us all, it has been most difficult for Emma, I think, who has a lot of my reclusive nature. Right from that awful day you came home with the news she closed herself up, refused even to discuss the possibility that cancer was going to take her mother from her. I know this gave you great pain, and so I wish you could see what I've seen during the past three days. Something vital is coming to life in her that has been buried for a long time. She's been painting again lately, I've noticed, and talking about going into a fine arts program.

We bought some flowers from a vendor's cart and came down to the lake. It was time to finish the rest of the letters. I read Chris and Emma your letter about leaving New York, and how you went for a walk in the park and met Reverend Mizu. Then I shared with them your last letter to me from China, and so now Chris and Emma discovered what you'd felt and what you knew in your heart, that Michael was still with you after he died, that you'd heard and seen him in the light and the water and the trees, and how you knew this was true of all of us, we are never really separate from one another and never would be. I remember that when you told me this I was happy for you but the truth was I didn't really understand. I had never felt that in nature, the presence of someone I cared for who wasn't there with me, not in all the marvels I'd seen. I want to feel it. I just don't know how. Probably it's not a matter of knowing how but more about just being patient.

My own birthday was only a week ago – I turned fifty-six, and now I find I'm not really sure what that means. My rational side knows that the earth has gone around the sun fifty-five times since I was born, and that this body of mine, as it must, is beginning to slow down, to enter its wintry season. And yet a part of me now knows this simply isn't true. I remember writing to you about how each of us is as old as the universe, but this is something else entirely, something that has nothing to do with physics or biology, and it was our children who helped me find it. Somewhere inside me a little boy is always picking berries among the poplars alongside the wheatfield with his mother. A shy, awkward young man is meeting the woman he will love for the rest of his life. An awestruck, terrified new father is holding his child, whom he has just watched being born.

A part of me lives in these moments forever, outside of time. This isn't a quantifiable fact science can pin down and explain away. It's simply a truth. My truth. I don't know if it's the same truth you discovered, but maybe it's a place to start.

I'm sitting now under an elm not far from the water. Chris and Emma have wandered down to the shore and rolled up the legs of their jeans to wade in the shallows. They're feeding the ducks with scraps of bread left over from our lunch. You know I don't approve of feeding wild animals but you'll be glad to hear I kept quiet about it on this occasion.

Just now one of the ducks got a little too aggressive about the bread and Emma was shrieking, jumping away. Chris was laughing, taking pictures with his newfangled phone camera. They are both so beautiful and so young, like two fledgling birds. Of course they'd be horrified if I told them that. I'm reminded of something I stumbled across on the internet the other day (the amazing, appalling internet that I'm happy didn't exist yet when we were writing letters all those years ago, the letters that were our own private internet), about the Australian bird known as the kookaburra. How their young stay around the nest for a full year after they hatch, to help their parents feed and care for the following year's nestlings. I don't know what this means, Martha, if anything. As always I'm relating some surprising, mysterious fact simply for the pleasure of talking to you.

The sun is starting to set now and the city skyline is turning to gold in the slanting light. I'm listening to the sound of the leaves softly stirring in the trees above me.

I'm going to close now and go join our kids by the water. Hope to meet you there.

Love forever,
James

ACKNOWLEDGEMENTS

I am deeply grateful to the following people for assistance, conversation, support, and wisdom: Sharon Wharton, Mary Wharton, William Thompson, Reverend Master Mugo White, the Edmonton Buddhist Meditation sangha, Reverend Master Aurelian Giles, C.P. Bird, the Toyomizu families in Hiroshima and Sendai, Xiao Jinghong, Prof. E. Agnarsson, Dr. J. Markowitz, Susan Toy, Sarah Lang, Paul Charest, Jennifer Keane Mackinnon, Jo-Anne Sieppert, and the late Ralph Vicinanza.

Made in the USA
Charleston, SC
21 January 2015